Tim BOWLER

GAME CHANGER

OXFORD

UNIVERSITY PRESS

OXFORD
UNIVERSITY PRESS

Great Clarendon Street, Oxford OX2 6DP
Oxford University Press is a department of the University of Oxford.
It furthers the University's objective of excellence in research, scholarship,
and education by publishing worldwide. Oxford is a registered trade mark of
Oxford University Press in the UK and in certain other countries

First published 2015

British Library Cataloguing in Publication Data

Data available

ISBN: 978-0-19-279415-4

1 3 5 7 9 10 8 6 4 2

Printed in Great Britain

Paper used in the production of this book is a natural,
recyclable product made from wood grown in sustainable forests.
The manufacturing process conforms to the environmental
regulations of the country of origin.

Also by

TiM BOWLER

FOR MY MOTHER WITH LOVE

CHAPTER 1

I'm trying to pretend yesterday didn't happen. Trouble is, they won't let me. I thought all I've got to do is keep out of the way, say nothing, and they'll see I'm safe; and I am safe, I'm totally safe, I just want to get on with my own stuff. I'm indoors most of the time anyway. I'm not called Mole for nothing. So what's to worry about? They could leave me alone and everything would be fine, but no. The email stares at me from the screen.

We gotta talk.

Then a phone number, a mobile. I check the email address again. Nothing that gives away a name, just random letters and numbers. I think back to yesterday, read the email again, click Reply and type an answer.

Nothing to talk about.

But that won't do. I delete the words and try again.

I won't say anything.

That feels wrong too. I listen to the sounds in the house: Dad washing up the supper things downstairs, Mum walking up and down the hall, talking on the phone. I'm just wondering where Meggie is when she knocks on my door.

'What you doing, big guy?' she calls.

I quickly cancel the unsent email and switch off the computer.

'Nothing much.'

She comes in and walks over. She's got a dressing gown on and a towel round her neck and her hair's wet from the shower. She puts a hand on my shoulder.

'Nothing much?' she says.

'Yeah.'

'Sounds like fun.'

She pulls up a chair next to me.

'You OK?' she says.

'Yeah.'

'Just switched off your computer?'

'Yeah.'

'Screen light's still on.'

I switch off the screen. She looks over my desk, picks up the top book from the pile.

'I know,' she says, glancing over it, 'nosy little sister.'

'I don't mind you being nosy.'

She studies the book cover.

'*Treasure Island*. You must have read this nine times, Mikey.'

More like twenty-nine times, but I don't tell Meggie that. She puts the book down again and turns to me.

'So what happened yesterday, big guy?'

'Nothing.'

'You were doing great,' she says. 'Mum and Dad are really pleased with the way you're trying to face things. But I didn't tell them how quiet you were coming back, how you were like . . . closed up. Was it that bad, where we went?'

'I chose the place, so it's my fault if it was.'

Meggie frowned.

'Maybe I should have fought you harder and taken you somewhere else. I was really worried when you told me where you wanted to go, Mikey, so noisy and crowded and everything, all the things that freak you out, normally. I thought you were being a bit overambitious.'

She's probably right—she usually is—but I was trying to show some bottle. I thought—I'll choose a tough place, a really tough place, all the things that scare the pants off me, and it'll be a real test for me to see if I can handle it, and I was handling it, sort of, till the stuff happened. I don't answer Meggie. Don't know what to say to her.

'Mikey?'

'Call me Mole like everyone else does.'

'Mum and Dad don't call you Mole, and I'm not going to either.'

I stare into Meggie's face. It's so hard to think of her as thirteen. She seems two years older than me rather than two years younger, but it's always been that way. It's only when she's got Lucy and her other mates round and they go all girlie that she seems her true age. I hear another knock at the door, then Mum puts her head round.

'Making hot drinks,' she says. 'Anybody interested?'

'Cocoa, please,' says Meggie.

'Mikey?'

'Hot chocolate, please.'

'Come down in ten minutes.'

And Mum closes the door. Meggie stands up, rubbing her hair with the towel.

'Mikey, you still haven't told me what went wrong yesterday.'

And I can't. I can't get Meggie involved, or Mum and Dad. I've got to think what to do, and I need time for that. It's complicated, really complicated. I'm hoping it'll be one of those things that'll go away if I don't do anything. Once they see I haven't said or done anything, they'll work out I'm no danger. I stare at the blank computer screen.

We gotta talk.

It's like the words are hiding there, even with the thing switched off. I feel Meggie's hand on my shoulder again.

'You were doing really well, Mikey,' she says. 'You managed half an hour at that place. That's good, that's really good. Maybe that's what scared you a bit. You're not used to it. But I was with you going and coming back, and we can do it again, tomorrow maybe, after school. We could go to the same place, so you get used to it, or maybe another place. Somewhere you feel really safe.'

I feel Meggie's hand leave my shoulder.

'See you downstairs,' she says.

And she's gone. I switch on the computer again, call up my emails, and there's another one: same meaningless address, but some new words.

Ring the number.

I stare at the message, call up the old one. The mobile number sits on the screen, waiting. I lean back in the chair. Outside in Denbury Close all is quiet. I stand up, walk to the window, and peer out. Darkness has fallen over the neat, familiar road. All my life it's seemed safe and reassuring; suddenly it doesn't. The clean cars, the well-tended gardens, the double garages, the immaculate houses—all seem hostile now. For the first time I see how many places there are to hide round here.

I make my way downstairs. They're all in the sitting room and their silence matches the silence in the close outside. We have our hot drinks. Dad does the crossword, Mum the Sudoku, Meggie texts her friends. I stare at the fire, the only thing making any noise right now.

'One for you here, Mikey,' says Dad suddenly.

I look round at him, but he's still studying the crossword. He reads out the clue.

'Name of the ship in *Treasure Island*. Ten letters.'

'*Hispaniola*.'

Mum chuckles, but says nothing.

'Thanks,' says Dad.

And they all carry on, Dad with his crossword, Mum with her Sudoku, Meggie with her texting. The fire goes slowly down. Back in my room later, as I make ready for bed, I switch on my computer again. There are four more emails from the same address. But it's just one message, repeated four times.

Talk to us and live mikey. Talk to anyone else and people gonna die. Including you xxx

CHAPTER 2

The darkness feels good. I burrow down deep in the bed. I like being called Mole. I know they mean it as an insult but I don't care. Moles do what I like doing. It's natural for them and it's natural for me. The thing is, if you don't have the fear, you can't understand the fear. That's what pisses me off about my shrink. He might have studied case histories of other people like me but he can't really understand what we go through unless he feels the fear himself.

And he doesn't. He's got no idea. He goes out of his house like almost everybody else does, and he never thinks twice about the terrifying openness of the world, the great, yawning void. He studies his cases and talks to his patients and gives us all his clever, wordy advice, and then he goes out and gets on with his brilliant life. I say 'us all' as if I know his other patients, but of course I don't. I never see them. Most of the time I don't even make it to his clinic.

Unless Meggie can get time off school and come with me. Usually he comes here, which is more expensive for Mum and Dad, and I feel bad about that, even though

6

they tell me it doesn't matter. But I guess it's not so much of a problem now that he's stopped coming so often. He insists I'm making progress and he doesn't need to see me so regularly, but he knows and I know that he's given up, because I'm making no progress at all, and the fear's still there, only it's bigger. It's turned into terror.

That's why books console me, specially novels by authors from another age, like Charles Dickens and Herman Melville. The people in their stories aren't real and the people who wrote them are long dead, so they don't feel real either. I'm never going to meet any of them outside of books, never going to have to deal with them face to face. So books are safe, and when I read, I feel safe too. Till I close the book.

The darkness folds around me, and now the warmth of the bed, and the silence outside in the close, and in my room. But the words don't go away. I see them against the blackness, just as they appeared on my computer screen, and they seem to speak aloud to me, like strange robotic voices in my ear.

'Talk to us and live, Mikey,' they say mechanically. 'Talk to anyone else and people gonna die. Including you.'

Yeah, right. I believe the second and third bit, so I'm keeping quiet there, but the first bit? Talk to us and live? I'm not stupid. I know what'll happen if I make contact with these people. So ringing won't help. Ringing will just bring them nearer, and they're near already. I can feel them close. I push my head out from the covers and peer about the dark room.

That's something that always chills me: how the darkness fades the longer you're in it. I don't want the darkness to fade; I want it to stay as black as possible, so it hides me really well, but it always eases, even after I've had my head under the covers. The room's clearer than the last time I saw it, and if it's clear for me, it could be clear for somebody else hiding here.

I stare round at the murky shapes, growing more visible by the minute. Nothing's moving and everything's still quiet outside the house. Doesn't feel right, though. I slip out of bed, pull my dressing gown on over my pyjamas, and peep round the side of the curtain into Denbury Close. Nothing moving down below, nothing I can see. I look up at the sky. Dull clouds, no stars or moon.

There should be much more darkness than this outside. I don't like it when everything's so clear. I leave the window and walk over to the bookshelves. I know where my books are by feel alone, every single one of them, but right now I can even see the writing on the spines, the books with larger lettering anyway. I wish I couldn't. This darkness is just too bright. I run my eye over the titles.

Oliver Twist.

I pull the book down. It's not my favourite Charles Dickens but never mind. I take it over to the armchair in the corner, slump down with my legs pulled into my chest, and hug the book in the darkness. After a while I hear footsteps on the landing: Meggie's, heading for the loo. Just as well I've got the light off or she'd see it and come and check I'm OK, and I'm not. Right now I'm a long way from OK. I open the book, stare at the blurry

8

text, but the only words I pick up are the ones chanting in my head. *People gonna die, people gonna die.*

Die, die, die.

I close the book, hug it again, then hear the click of the bathroom door and Meggie's footsteps once more, only they're not heading back to her room: they're heading this way. A pause outside my door, then it quietly opens and I see her head appear in the gap. But she doesn't see me. She's staring towards the bed. It takes her a few moments to realize I'm not there, then she turns, quickly, as if in a panic.

'I'm over here, Meggie.'

She sees me curled up on the chair.

'Mikey,' she says, with obvious relief, 'what you doing sitting in the dark?'

'What you doing checking me out?'

She closes the door behind her and walks over.

'I often check to see if you're sleeping,' she says.

'I didn't know.'

'That's because you're always sleeping when I look in.'

'So why do you check, then?'

'I check when I'm worried about you.'

'But if I'm always sleeping when you look in,' I say, 'there's obviously nothing to worry about.'

I don't mention the times I've sat here in the darkness on the nights when she didn't check.

'I just know you often don't sleep,' she says. 'So I'm guessing you curl up on that chair and think and worry, even if I haven't seen you doing it.'

'You don't know I do that.'

9

'You're doing it now.'

I don't answer.

'What are you hugging to yourself?' she says suddenly.

I hold out the book. She takes it and stares at the jacket.

'Can't read this,' she says eventually. 'Too dark.'

'Don't put on the light.'

'I wasn't going to.'

She hands it back to me and stands there, looking down. Yet again I wonder at her being thirteen. It's almost like Mum standing next to me. She reaches out suddenly and ruffles my hair. Like Mum does.

'It'll be OK, Mikey,' she says, and she quietly leaves the room. I wait till I hear her own door click, then pull the book back into my chest and close my eyes.

'Die, die, die,' say the words in my head.

CHAPTER 3

'Mikey, come out of there.'

I don't answer, and I don't need to. All Dad's got to do is open the wardrobe door. It's not like it's locked or anything, and he knows that. He tries again, though.

'Mikey, it's half-past seven in the morning and we shouldn't have to keep going through this.'

I glance round the inside of the wardrobe. I've got so used to its musty smell down the years it feels as normal as the hanging clothes brushing the top of my head in the dark. If the wood wasn't so hard and the space so cramped, I'd sleep in here every night. The door opens suddenly and there's Dad's face, and Mum's too, looking in at me. They're trying not to be angry, but I know they are. I hate making them like this.

'Mikey,' says Mum, 'you can overcome this. You know you can, because you've done it before.'

I've also stayed all day and all night in the wardrobe before, but there's no point reminding her of that; and she is right. I've made it out of here quite a few times— just not often enough to keep us all happy. They're still watching me, confusion on their faces, along with the anger and frustration. I want to help them so much, I want to see the pain in their eyes disappear, but it's no good. I can feel the old familiar sweat over my body, the coldness round my neck, the shudder in my stomach. I feel for a book to clutch and realize with horror that I didn't bring one with me when I shut myself in here— and I always bring a book. Even *Oliver Twist* would have done, but I think I left it on the chair.

'Here it is,' says Meggie's voice.

She appears from the left, just behind Mum and Dad, and she's holding a book, but it's not *Oliver Twist*: it's *Moby Dick*, much better. Herman Melville should get me out of here. I hold my hand out for it, but Meggie shakes her head and stays out of reach.

'Meggie, that's blackmail,' I say.

'You don't need it, big guy,' she says. 'I'll give it to you if you really want, but you don't need it.'

I scramble out of the wardrobe, stand up in front of them, then grab *Moby Dick* from Meggie.

'I do need it,' I say.

I stare down at the familiar picture of the great whale, the tiny boat, the men at the oars, the harpoonist, the heaving sea; then feel a hand on my arm. It's Mum's.

'Let's get you to school today, Mikey,' she says.

'Yes.'

'Mr Cable's back today, isn't he?'

'Yes.'

'So that's a good reason for going in.'

I can think of a few hundred for not going in, but I just give Mum a hug. She moves a little awkwardly against me.

'What's wrong?' I say.

'You're holding that book at a funny angle and it's digging into me.'

I start to pull back, but she draws me closer.

'I still want the hug,' she says, 'with or without the book.'

I try to adjust it so she doesn't feel it.

'That's better,' she says.

I feel Dad and Meggie watching us, and it suddenly hits me again: the silence all around. It's like nothing's happening out in Denbury Close, and nothing in here either, like we're all leading soundless lives. I think of the other houses and wonder if they're just as quiet inside, and I suddenly wish Mum and Dad would listen to the radio in the mornings, or Meggie would put some of her rubbish music on.

But it's probably just me. Silence and space go together, like two parts of the void. Dad gives me a fatherly pat. I go on holding Mum, but there's a second pat from Dad, and I know I've got to let go. I hate all these games as much as they do. I wonder what they'd think if they knew the bigger game I've got to play now. I drop the book on the bed and step back from Mum. She smiles.

'Let's make it a school day, Mikey.'

'Rather than a wardrobe day.'

'Exactly.'

She takes me by the hand and leads me out through the door and down the landing towards the bathroom.

'I can do this bit, Mum.'

She lets go at once.

'Of course, darling.'

She walks back towards the door of my room. I see Dad and Meggie waiting there, watching, and for the thousandth time in my life, I feel the old guilt dump itself on me, like it wants to squash me into the floor. Maybe one day it will. Mum walks past the others and sets off down the stairs.

'Breakfast in twenty minutes,' she calls over her shoulder.

Dad follows, with a glance in my direction. I flash him a smile and he manages one back before he disappears from view. Meggie's still standing in my doorway. I look grumpily over at her.

'What are you gawping at?' I mutter.

She walks slowly up to me and stops. She's already dressed for school. For all I know she's had breakfast, got her bag packed, maybe spent the last twenty minutes on her phone or online, hooking up with her mates. She gives me a smile.

'See you downstairs, big guy.'

And she turns away. I dive into the bathroom, rush through showering, dry off, hurry back to my room, get dressed, switch on my computer. I've been dreading this moment. All through the night I've been feeling the thing pulling me, because I know it'll have more messages, more warnings, more death threats probably, and all through the night I've been resisting, or rather huddling inside the wardrobe and pretending it'll go away if I just ignore it. But I can't ignore it now, specially now I've got to go to school. I can't leave the house without reading everything they've said.

14

But to my surprise there are no more messages, from them or anyone else. I stare at the blank screen. I'm almost disappointed, not because I want more messages but because it cost me so much last night to stop myself running to switch on the computer. I lean back in the chair, watching the screen, then, on an impulse, delete every single one of the messages that have come in, switch off the computer, and make my way downstairs to join the others.

CHAPTER 4

I get to the car OK, not sure how, maybe through Meggie holding my hand and chivvying me like I'm a kid, which I guess I sort of am, and then I'm inside and on the back seat and the door's closed, and Meggie's next to me on the other seat, fastening my safety belt.

'I can do that,' I mumble.

She lets me, and we set off, Mum driving. Dad swivels round.

'What are you doing?' I ask him.

'I'm not doing anything,' he says.

'You're staring at me.'

'What makes you think you're worth staring at, Mikey?'

'You're checking me out.'

'No, I'm not. I'm checking Meggie out.'

'What for?'

'She's my daughter and I'm starting to like her.'

'Starting?' says Meggie.

Mum laughs. I look at Meggie, who's also laughing, then Dad.

'You were staring at me, not Meggie,' I say.

Dad turns pointedly to Meggie.

'Looking at her now, Mikey. That OK?'

I reach for the car door. Can't help it, even though we're moving fast. Meggie's hand catches my wrist, just ahead of Dad's.

'Let go,' I say.

Neither of them do. Mum slows the car to walking pace. I glare round at them, then at the overwhelming space, the bright empty thing that's not empty at all but hugely, horribly full; and yet this car seems somehow worse, small though it is, closed in though it is. Maybe it's my emptiness that's filling it. They're still holding my wrist, both of them, but Meggie strokes my arm now.

'Come on, big guy, easy.'

'Sorry,' I murmur, 'sorry.'

'Nothing to be sorry about,' says Mum, speeding up again.

I glance round at them all, then grunt.

'Getting good at this, aren't you?'

'What do you mean?' says Dad.

'Team Mole,' I mutter. 'How to handle the nutter.'

I didn't mean to be sarcastic. OK, I did. But I hate myself for it. Meggie eases my hand from the door and pulls it into her lap.

'You're not a nutter, Mikey,' she says, 'you're just high maintenance.'

'I give you days off sometimes.'

'Not very often.'

'Fair enough.'

Meggie smiles at me, then lowers her voice.

'Mikey, let's go back to that place again after school.'

I look away, out of the window.

'You did really well there,' she says. 'I was so proud of you.'

'You said you were worried about me because I went all quiet on the way home.'

'That's why I want us to go back there,' she says. 'So you can get over whatever it was that didn't work last time. Because you almost made it all the way through. I left you on your own there and you did great.'

'You don't know that. You didn't see me. Not when I was on my own.' I turn back to her suddenly. 'Unless you were watching me in secret.'

'I wasn't watching you in secret, Mikey,' she says. 'You know I wouldn't do that. I gave you a promise and I wouldn't break it.'

That's true. I didn't really doubt her. She's the most honest person I know.

'So I don't know what you did when I left you,' she says, 'but you stayed there all by yourself, and then you came back—OK, a bit earlier than we agreed—but you found me, and you managed all that on your own, and I was really proud of you. But then you went quiet on the way home and I could just tell you weren't right.'

I feel Mum and Dad listening, but holding back. Meggie moves closer.

'So let's go back there after school,' she says. 'It's a safe place. I know I wasn't sure about it when you first suggested it, because of it being so noisy and crowded and everything, but you did really well there, much better than I thought you would, and if we go back again, you

18

can maybe get over whatever it was that freaked you out last time.'

Dad speaks at last, in an unconvincingly casual voice.

'Where did you guys go the other day?'

Meggie gives him a look and he backs off straight-away.

'OK, OK,' he says, 'your secret, that's fine. Mum and I don't need to know. Long as it's safe.'

'It's boringly safe,' says Meggie.

'And legal.'

'Boringly legal.'

Meggie gives me a smile, but I can't manage one back because we've pulled into the school gate. The first hurdle's the space between the door of the car and the door of the building, but it's Team Mole straight into action again. Mum parks as close as she can and Meggie's round my side quicker than I can get out, not that I'm hurrying. I see her smiling in at me, and behind her on both sides other kids arriving. I hate them so much, or rather I hate what they can do, strolling in like that, free as a breeze. But Meggie's got the door open now, and Mum and Dad are checking round, smiling that pretend-smile that says everything's cool: you're cool, we're cool, this is cool. Only none of it is. And we all know it.

'Have a good day, sweethearts,' says Mum.

I get out of the car. Meggie closes the door, blows Mum and Dad a kiss, and hooks a hand inside my arm. I shoot a glance at her. She's only started doing this lately—maybe she's desperate to keep me from running away—but I've told her not to do it, and she's got to stop: there's two guys from my year watching. She picks up my glance, takes her hand away, then leans close.

'They're not watching you, Mikey.'

'They are.'

'They're not.'

'So who are they watching?'

Meggie shakes her head.

'Me, you idiot.'

I check round but the boys have moved off. I look back at Meggie.

'Don't be so surprised, big guy,' she says.

I'm not surprised really. I've noticed it before. Like I've said, she always seems older than me, even though she's two years younger, and I guess the boys in my year feel it too; and she is good-looking. Even I can see that.

'I'm not surprised,' I say.

I realize for the first time that Mum and Dad have driven off without me noticing. Seems there's a lot I'm missing right now; either that or I'm noticing the wrong things. Maybe I've spent so much time trying not to be noticed it's messed up what I think I see. Meggie's touching me again, just a little coaxing nudge, and I move with her up the steps towards the school entrance. Couple of her mates waiting inside, and they've seen us, but I can't be worrying about them. I'm too busy trying to get inside and away from the gaping hole of daylight, and trying not to show it.

But we're in now, and the entrance passage closes lovingly around us. That's one good thing about old-fashioned posh schools like this one with their centuries of tradition: they've got these ancient buildings with lots of dark corridors and small rooms. Maybe it's the wood panelling or the lighting or the poky windows they haven't got round to updating, but they give me places I can feel less frightened in: not proper places for a mole to burrow away in, but better than nothing. You can't ever really hide here, though. Home's the only place I can do that, and it doesn't even work there sometimes, and I don't just mean hide myself from view. I mean hide what I am. But I'm inside the school now and that's one challenge over. There are plenty more waiting, I know that already, because there always are, and that's even without what happened the other day. I glance at Meggie.

'I'll take it from here,' I say.

She looks back at me, then gives a smile.

'See you later, big guy,' she says.

And she and her mates are gone.

CHAPTER 5

No, it's not just about hiding myself. It's about hiding the truth. I have to keep secrets from everybody, even Mum and Dad, even Meggie, specially Meggie. She loves me too much already and if I told her everything, she'd worry so much about me she wouldn't have a life. She'd be with me all the time, checking how I am, and I can't let her do that, specially when it wouldn't help anyway. Because the point is, I have to cope with the really weird stuff on my own.

The average weird stuff—well, everyone knows I've got that. I don't mind them knowing. I've learnt to live with it. The nickname Mole came like nature designed it for me. Started in my first year at this school with the other kids messing with the surname, like they do with a new boy, and since Molyneux sounds a bit like Mole, or has a bit of Mole in it, they went with that for a while. Then they picked up that I don't like going out of the house and I hate bright places and keep missing school or going in and then getting fetched by Mum or Dad and taken home, and the nickname fitted even better, and now it's stuck.

But I don't care. I've got bigger stuff to worry about now, specially after what happened the other day. The first hurdle, though, is getting to Room Eighteen for Session One. Because that's one of the challenges in this place, and any other place, for that matter: knowing how to get from A to B without unleashing the terror, and without other people knowing I've got it. Mostly I manage this, I think, even with Meggie, but I pay the price. People see the weird behaviour and they guess it could be something to do with fear, but they're not sure. There's part of them thinking: what if it's not fear? What if it's just attention-seeking?

Nobody's ever said that out loud to me. Mum and Dad haven't anyway, or Meggie, or my shrink, but I see it in their faces, and people at school show it plain as you like, and they don't just show it: I pick up snide comments, the sharp edge of things they say to each other when they think I can't hear, or maybe when they think I can. I hear other things too, apart from attention-seeking: lying's one of them; paranoid's another. There's more, lots more. They basically all mean the same thing.

Fake.

So I try to hide the terror from people. Don't want them adding coward to the list as well, though maybe they already do, and I can't blame them if that's true, because I know deep down that I am a coward really. I freak out at the slightest thing, and now there's the problem of two days ago to add to the mix. But right now I've got to forget about that and focus on getting to Room Three for Registration (easy), and then Room Eighteen for Session One (scary). OK, easy bit first. Long dark corridor, all the way to Room Three, and fortunately no sign of any trouble.

'Hey, Mole.'

Shit, Ringo and Jeb. Not dangerous but I could do without them. They fall into step, one either side of me. Ringo gives me a nudge.

'How you doing, Mole?'

'Fine.'

'Didn't expect to see you in today.'

'Why not?'

'I thought you only came out after dark.'

'Don't know what you mean.'

I do, but never mind. Jeb chips in.

'Sun's shining, Mole.'

'Never noticed.'

'It's that big bright round thing in the sky.'

I say nothing. They keep pace with me, staying close.

'Done your Latin homework?' says Ringo.

I don't bother answering. He knows I have and I know he hasn't.

'I couldn't find the Latin for dickhead,' he says.

'*Wankus maximus*.'

'What?'

'*Wankus maximus*.' I glance at him. 'Look it up.'

They stay with me all the way to Room Three, then run in to join the others. I check through the door and see Nip watching me. Another problem I'm not sure how to deal with. The whole class is there, apart from me, but no sign of Mr Cable yet. Then I hear his voice behind me.

'Michael Molyneux,' he says, 'nice to see you.'

I turn and look up at him.

'Nice to see you too, sir,' I say.

The words feel creepy coming out of my mouth, but I can't help it. I mean them. I hated it when he was off sick. We got stuck with Mrs Winslow and she hates me. Mr Cable smiles.

'*Wankus maximus,*' he murmurs. 'Nice one, Michael.'

Shit, I can't believe he was following and heard me. He smiles again, then walks into the classroom and over to his desk. I hurry in after him and take my place next to Nip. The eyes of the class fix on me, but I'm used to being weird to them and right now I've got more important things to worry about. Mr Cable calls for attention and the eyes settle back on him. Well, most of them do. Some still dart little glances in my direction. I force myself to think about Room Eighteen.

I've been through the route in my head, the usual way from here. It normally goes OK, but today's sunny, as Ringo so kindly reminded me, and that makes it darker in terms of the terror. So I've got my coat ready in case it's Plan B. Mr Cable starts the register. The eyes flicker back my way, not all at once, just little glances fluttering like tiny birds. Mr Cable goes through the names, makes a couple of announcements, then dismisses us. There's a scraping of chairs and people start to move. Nip stays in his seat but twists round to face me. I look warily at him.

'How you doing, mate?' he says.

'OK.'

'Yeah?'

'Fine, I'm great.'

He looks me over with that expression that always mystifies me: an expression of trust, like he actually believes what I just told him. I don't get it. I'm obviously not OK, not fine, not great, or whatever I said to him. I'm a wacko. Even I know that. So how Nip can see me as a friend and not as a nutter, like everybody else does here, apart from Meggie, is beyond me. I just don't get it. Even I don't like me. But Nip? It's not even as though he sees the weird stuff but doesn't care about it. It's like he actually doesn't notice it in the first place, like he doesn't know it's there, but how can anyone miss it? How can he see me as a friend and not a basket case? Fills me with guilt when he looks at me like this, and now he makes it worse.

'How's Meggie?' he says.

I don't want to talk about Meggie. I really don't want to talk about Meggie. Because we've had this conversation before, Nip and me, and although I know he means it as a joke, I know where this is going and I can't handle it right now. But I've got to answer him somehow.

'Meggie's great,' I say.

'I know she's great,' says Nip, 'but how is she?'

'She's fine. She's OK.'

Nip glances round the classroom. Still quite a few people hanging about, but they're all talking and no one's interested in us. Even so, he leans close and lowers his voice.

'So what about my idea?' he says.

'Not now, Nip.'

'Come on, mate. We've talked about it before.'

'The answer's no.'

'Straight swap. Your sister for mine.'

'No.'

26

'Meggie for Nell. It'll be fun.'

'No.'

'Just for a day.'

He's grinning at his joke. He loves running with this. He just never notices that I hate it. Meggie's so special I think I'd die without her. I can't make jokes about losing Meggie, even for a day. But I can't be horrible to Nip either, not when he insists on being my friend. He goes on riffing.

'It could work,' he says. 'Meggie's thirteen going on seventeen, Nell's seventeen going on thirteen. They've both got big personalities. They've got a lot in common.'

'No, they haven't!'

I didn't mean to snap at him. It just came rushing out.

'Sorry, mate,' I say quickly. 'I didn't mean to over-react. I'm just a bit protective with Meggie.'

'Some people might say it's the other way round,' says Nip.

He's right there. I look at him, feeling bad for cutting him up when he didn't mean anything. He shrugs suddenly, the joke well and truly over.

'Actually, Nell's driving us nuts, man,' he says.

I've heard this enough times. I don't want to hear it again. But I can't stop him after my outburst.

'She's worse than she was even a month ago,' he says. 'Screaming rows with Mum and Dad. Not with me, though. Crazy, isn't it? She's a bit like Meggie is with you, protective towards me, big-sisterly, but Mum and Dad? Jesus, do they get it? Slamming doors, storming out, smashing things. We don't know where she is half the time. She just takes off for the day and sometimes the night as well, then rolls up again at home like it's all cool. Hasn't been in school for weeks. You must have noticed. Don't get me wrong. We all love her to bits, but she's driving us mental. So yeah.' Nip looks hard at me. 'Hang on to Meggie, OK? Because she's gold dust, mate.'

I didn't need to be told the last bit. I look away, unsure what to say. To my relief, Mr Cable pipes up from the desk.

'Session One! Too many people dawdling!'

I look over at him gratefully and stand up. Nip does the same and we walk out into the corridor with the other stragglers. I stop by the door, trying to think of an excuse I haven't used with Nip before. He looks at me, innocent of all this, as usual.

'You coming?' he says.

'In a minute. Listen.' I lower my voice. 'I've just got to ask Mr Cable something.'

'I'll wait for you down the corridor.'

'No, you go on ahead. I'll see you there.'

'OK.'

I wait till Nip and the others have disappeared, then check Mr Cable isn't watching, and hurry off the other way.

CHAPTER 6

The corridor's crowded, and that's good for the moment, but now there's a problem with kids from my Latin set bustling towards me from other form groups.

'Going the wrong way, Mole,' says Jamie.

Luckily they're all as late as I am, so they carry on past without further comment, but I've been spotted now and I was hoping to avoid that. Got to keep moving, though, and fast, or I'll be in trouble with Mrs Reed again for not getting to Latin on time. Round the corridor only to find more latecomers hurrying towards me.

'Room Eighteen, Mole,' says Billy.

'See you there,' I mutter.

'Other way, Mole.'

I take no notice and keep going, but check back as I slip round the corner. Billy's stopped and he's watching me, frowning. I hate all this stupid pantomime. There's nothing wrong with Billy, any more than Jamie, and most of the others, and I don't blame them for not getting me. How could they? Even Meggie doesn't get me, and my shrink certainly doesn't. He talks like he's worked it all out, like there's a root cause to the problem, a trigger that sets off the fear, and if I can just find the root cause, the trigger, then I can find strategies around it.

And I suppose he should know. I mean, he's got a name that fits him almost as well as mine fits me. Braine, Mr Braine. Apart from the wobbly spelling, it's perfect for someone who's supposed to know what's going on inside people's heads, and he thinks he does, oh yeah, he's dead confident about that, only it's all bollocks, it's big, crazy bollocks, it's *wankus maximus*, call it what you like, because there's something even shrinks like Mr Braine don't get, and Mum and Dad and Meggie don't get, and the other kids here don't get, and dear old Nip'll never get, bless his heart—and that's the simple truth that sometimes a fear just exists by itself. The fear exists, end of. And when it's bad, it's more than fear.

It's terror.

And that exists too, by itself, end of. No root cause, no trigger. You're born terrified, you live terrified, you probably die terrified. I don't know about that bit yet. I guess I'll find out when the time comes. Maybe I'm wrong. Maybe the terror will go away, or I'll find a strategy, like Mr Braine says, and the terror will downgrade to fear, and then to anxiety, and then to a manageable kind of worry, and then that'll slip away too, and I'll find I'm cruising through life and everything's cool. Maybe that'll happen. But I'm not holding my breath. And right now, all I can think of is Room Eighteen, and the vice closing round my heart.

No more kids hurrying the other way, and only a few in the corridor now, late like me, ducking into classrooms. I'm round the next corner and tearing down the east section of the quadrangle. Don't like this bit with the open daylight to my right and that bright horrible sun. I keep to the wall on my left, classroom windows flashing by with faces peering out at me as I pass, and now I'm at the bottom where the caretaker's room is, and the store cupboards with his gear. I cut left, through the double doors and down the passageway to the side door to the playground, and then I stop.

Through the glass panel I gaze out at the bright empty playground, far brighter than it should be on a November morning. I ought to be used to this. I feel like I've been here a hundred thousand times before; and a hundred thousand times I've hesitated, just like this. The only thing that's certain is that it would have been worse if I'd gone the direct way like Nip and the others and hit the playground from the door in the opposite wing. That's quicker through the building but further across the playground, so there's way more exposure to the light. I stare across at the other wing, and then at Room Eighteen, in its prefab hut.

A tiny island in a sea of terror called the playground, but I'm nearer from this door, no distance at all really. I take a couple of breaths, try to pep myself up with the usual words. It's easy, dead easy, piece of cake, one small step for a boy. Yeah, right. One small step for a boy, one giant leap for a wacko like me, and a leap of terror at that. I take another couple of breaths, mark out the ground with my eyes.

'Fourteen paces,' I mutter. 'That's all it is. You've counted it enough times. So do it. Just do it.'

The sun grows brighter. So does the playground.

'OK, Plan B.'

I pull my coat over my head, duck, push open the door, pelt over the playground, eyes down. Even under my coat the ground seems to glow but I go on counting paces, willing myself on before the black vice squeezes me into nothing. I'm five paces in when it comes, bastard black thing, ramming me inside myself. I close my eyes and go on running, praying my feet won't stumble, but it's not my feet that fail. The prefab knocks me over first. I must have been taking bigger steps. I was only up to thirteen paces. I fall back, head spinning, and sprawl on the ground.

I pick myself up again, the coat half-wrapped round my head, and feel my way to the door into the little cloakroom with the coats. From the other side of the inner wall I hear Mrs Reed quipping with somebody, then a burst of laughter from the class. I tear my coat away and hang it up, and try to calm my breathing. But I'm shaking badly. I wait a few seconds, listening for sounds inside the room, but the laughter's gone and silence has spread. Then the door to the classroom opens and I see Mrs Reed's face.

'Michael,' she says quietly. 'I thought I heard somebody out here.'

'I'm sorry I'm late again, miss.'

I wait for the ticking off, but it doesn't come. The silence goes on instead, from Mrs Reed, and from the class behind her, their faces hidden by the wall. She speaks suddenly.

'Pick up your bag, Michael,' she says. 'You've dropped it by the door.'

I don't even remember carrying it. I reach down and pick it up, then make for the door. Mrs Reed holds out an arm and I stop. She's watching me closely, not in an unkind way, but I'm feeling awkward. I keep thinking of Ringo, Billy, Jamie, Nat, Briny, and the others, and Nip, of course, still hidden by the wall, still silent, like they're waiting for Mrs Reed to speak so they can listen in. She steps out of the classroom suddenly and closes the door after her. The silence goes on in the room beyond.

'They can't hear us, Michael,' she says softly.

I think she's wrong, but there's nothing I can do about that. I try to work out what Mrs Reed wants. I've got to be in trouble for something. Then she smiles.

'I'm worried about you, Michael,' she says.

'Why, Miss?'

'Because you look frightened.'

CHAPTER 7

I've got to think how to play this. I don't want Mrs Reed finding things out, or anyone else for that matter. I keep thinking of that message. *Talk to us and live mikey. Talk to anyone else and people gonna die. Including you.* I look back at Mrs Reed and manage a shrug.

'I always look frightened, Miss. I've got that kind of face.'

She's not even half-fooled by this. She just shakes her head.

'I've seen you looking lots of things, Michael,' she says. 'I've seen you looking anxious, wary, shy, awkward.' She pauses. 'And also kind, friendly, and fun to be around.'

I wasn't expecting the last three.

'I've also seen you frightened,' she adds.

'Like I say, Miss, I've got that kind of face.'

'But never this frightened,' she says.

I hear voices inside the classroom, Ringo's and Jeb's, jokey voices, talking about me, I'm guessing, though I can't catch the words, and now others are pitching in, and there's some laughter. Mrs Reed takes no notice of it.

'Michael, if it's none of my business,' she says, 'then

fair enough, but if you're in any kind of trouble, I hope you'll talk to somebody about it. You can certainly speak to me if there's ever anything wrong, and you know you can always speak to Mr Cable.'

I don't want to speak to anyone about it. I want to go away and burrow into my wardrobe, and think about it on my own. I'm still hoping it'll go away if I do nothing and stay out of reach. They'll soon realize I'm no danger to them. If I open my mouth and blab, then there'll be casualties, so the last thing I want is teachers getting involved.

'Thanks, Miss,' is all I can say.

Mrs Reed opens the door again and stands aside. The talk and laughter fall away and I walk into a silent classroom, all eyes upon me. Nip gives me a wink. Not sure what that's supposed to mean, if anything. I sit down next to him, pull my books out of my bag and spread them over the desk. Mrs Reed closes the door and starts the lesson like nothing's happened and we haven't just been having a private conversation outside. I glance round the room, checking Ringo, Jeb, Billy, Jamie, Nat, and the others.

No one looks back. It's heads down everywhere now, books open, pages turning, eyes searching for the spot. Page twenty, where we left off last time, with Hannibal about to make his move against the Roman army at the Battle of Cannae. I know this story already. I read ahead one time inside the wardrobe, with a torch, and got interested, and then I did some research on the computer. I love the way Hannibal clobbered the Romans. Wish I could do the same with my enemies. I check the boys again. No eyes moving in my direction, but I see Briny looking over, and some of the other girls. Nip, as usual, doesn't seem to notice any of this. He just leans close and whispers to me.

'What's going on, mate?' he says. 'You and Mrs Reed talking outside.'

'Nip,' calls Mrs Reed. 'Start the translation, can you? Second paragraph from the top.'

I glance at her. Clever move. It was probably meant to pull Nip back on task, but it's helped me too, so I'm grateful, even if she never intended it. She's still watching Nip, like she's determined not to catch my eye. Nip struggles through the first few sentences, mangling the translation horribly, then looks up at Mrs Reed.

'Carry on, Nip,' she says.

'Was it right, Miss?'

'We'll clean up the devastation later. Carry on.'

He fumbles on, stops, stares at the text, goes on staring.

'Anybody?' says Mrs Reed.

Jacintha puts her hand up.

'Go ahead, Jacintha,' says Mrs Reed.

Jacintha ploughs confidently on, and that's when I see the figures through the window: a guy and a girl, seventeen or eighteen years old, and no mistaking who they are. They've climbed up the hidden side of the wall on the far side of the playground, and they're staring across at Room Eighteen or, to be more precise, at me. No question. They're looking straight at me. They don't stay long. They just watch for a bit, make sure I've noticed them, then drop down the other side of the wall out of sight, out of everyone's sight, it seems, except mine. I'm pretty sure no one else spotted them. Certainly no one's said anything. Jacintha's voice breaks back into my mind and I realize she's been translating all the time. But I can't think about Hannibal and the Battle of Cannae any more. The moment the lesson ends, I'm out of my chair and heading for the door. Nip catches me up and grabs me by the arm, others watching as they push past us.

'Hold on, mate,' he says.

'Can't stop, Nip.'

'But—'

'I've got see Mr Cable about something.'

I hate lying to Nip. He always believes me and that just makes it worse. But it's no good. I don't want to talk, even to Nip. I want to be on my own so I can think.

'Meet up at break?' he says. 'Outside the gym?'

'OK.'

I hurry towards the door, but now Mrs Reed's blocking the way. She smiles at me.

'Remember what I said earlier, Michael.'

And she turns back to her desk. I make my way out, Nip close behind me, full of questions.

'What's she talking about?' he says. 'What did she say to you earlier?'

We're in the cloakroom now, but there are others still hanging round, taking their time so they can hear my answer. I reach for my coat.

'Don't know what she means.'

Most of the others run off but Nip doesn't, and Jamie goes on loitering by the outer door with Billy. They're facing outwards like they're watching Jade and Julie walk across the playground, which they probably are, but they're listening too. I pull my coat on and turn to Nip.

'Listen, I've got to go back in to see Mrs Reed.'

'You just said you've got to see Mr Cable.'

'I've got to see Mrs Reed too.'

Nip stares at me, confusion on his face.

'He's lying,' says Billy, still staring out into the playground. 'Wouldn't waste your time with him, Nip. Come on, Jamie.'

And the two boys run off after Jade and Julie, leaving Nip and me in the cloakroom. I hear the scrape of a chair next door, then Mrs Reed's face appears again.

'All right, boys?' she says.

'Mikey wants to see you about something,' says Nip, and, without another word, he runs off across the playground too. Mrs Reed looks at me.

'What can I do for you, Michael?'

I hesitate. Now that Nip's gone, I don't need an excuse to hang around.

'Yes?' says Mrs Reed.

I look away towards the playground. Just for once it seems inviting.

'Michael?'

I turn back to Mrs Reed. She frowns.

'You know where I am, Michael,' she says, and she turns back into the classroom.

I walk to the door that opens on to the playground and stand there. In the classroom nearby I hear Mrs Reed writing something on the board for her next class. I've got to move quick, before her pupils come streaming across the playground. I can't handle them as well as the daylight. No time to shove my coat over my head. They'll be here any moment. I'll just have to face the glare. I dive out of the door and race across the playground.

Three steps in and I feel the brightness stabbing my face. Another three and the light's turned to darkness in its usual perversion of the sun, and I've got the first big scream welling up inside me. I hold it in somehow and stagger on, and here at last is the door to the main building. Through it and inside, and a moment later I'm leaning against the wall just down from the caretaker's office; and there's Mr Fenby himself, chewing in the doorway.

'Mr Mole,' he says placidly, 'you look out of breath.'

I see kids from the year below heading towards me. They clatter past and through the door, and on across the playground towards Room Eighteen and their lesson with Mrs Reed. I leave Mr Fenby chewing and hurry down the corridor, left at the end, and down towards the ancient library. At least this is one room I like. I'm yearning for its dullness. I don't care about the complaints from parents since Mrs Bentley started taking our English lessons in there. They can grumble as much as they want. The old classroom was miserable anyway and the desks and chairs were falling to pieces, but the library . . .

The library's one of the oldest parts of the school, and it's only got windows down one side, and they're small and narrow, and though they open on to the back of the rugby field, there are high plane trees just outside that block the light even more, so if you sit well back from the windows like I always do, it's a good place to be—

plus there's all the novels here that I could ever want, and the librarians let me borrow more than the other kids, because they know I'm keen. I can't wait to get there now, specially after seeing those two faces peering over the wall at me. I need to calm down a bit. I see the library door at the end of the corridor, hear the sound of the class inside, and Mrs Bentley's voice calling them to order. Then a new sound.

The fire bell.

CHAPTER 8

A moment later the door of the library bursts open and Tina and Steffi burst out, followed by more of the class. It's only a drill—I remember Mr Cable mentioning it now at Registration—but I could do without it because I know where we've got to assemble. I stand aside and let the others pile out. They push past and bustle off down the corridor. I glance through into the library and see Mrs Bentley bringing up the rear, wheezing. She catches sight of me and waves me on after the others. I take no notice and wait for her.

'Go on ahead, Michael,' she says.

'What if you were in trouble,' I say, 'overcome by the smoke or something?'

'Very gallant of you, Michael,' she says. 'Now hurry along.'

She shepherds me towards the door and we set off together down the corridor. Having just escaped the daylight, I'm dreading the next bit. I almost wish there was real smoke I could hide in rather than face what's waiting for me outside the building. If I had a breathing mask, I'd definitely choose the smoke. But Mrs Bentley keeps me moving and somehow we end up outside on the school forecourt, together with the rest of my English group, and all the other classes, chattering and laughing like this is all a bit of fun.

Only it's hell for me. I stay in my class row like I'm meant to, huddled near the back, trying to find a shadow, but there's none. I'm aching for Mr Pearson to stand in front of us, do his little lecture, and send us back inside the building, but he's waiting for a couple more classes to arrive. I stay where I am and keep quiet. Nobody's talking to me but that's OK. I don't want conversation. I just want to go back inside. Steffi and Julie look round at me.

'You OK, Mole?' says Steffi.

'Fine.'

'You've got your head down.'

I'm crouched over too. She might as well say it.

'You're crouched over too.'

I manage to straighten up a bit, but I can't keep it for long, not with the sky so bright. I'm soon bending over again. Don't know why they're bringing this up. It's not like they haven't seen it before.

'I've got a stomach ache,' I mutter.

It's meant to be a joke, but Julie just gives me a little pat.

'Do you want us to go and get the nurse?' she says.

I look up at her.

'No, thanks.'

I think of those two figures again, the ones who looked over the wall, and then their friends, the ones I didn't see, but who can't be far away. I glance round best

I can, check out the road beyond the school gate. Lots of people walking past, and quite a few standing round, watching our fire drill. God knows what for. Maybe they think something's happening for real. There's nobody I recognize, certainly not the two I saw earlier. Doesn't mean they're not close, though. I've got a feeling they are. Mrs Bentley's walking down the row, checking we're all here, and the other teachers are doing the same with their groups. Meggie turns up at my side.

'OK, big guy?' she says.

'You should be with your group.'

'I got permission to come over. You OK?'

'Fine.'

But Meggie's not fooled as easily as Steffi.

'What's up?' she says. 'Something happened?'

'I'm out here, aren't I? Daylight's happened.'

'Something else, I mean.'

'Nothing else has happened.'

'You sure, Mikey?'

'I'm OK. Don't fuss over me.'

I see people watching me again: Julie, Steffi, other people from my class. Mrs Bentley's at the front of the group now, and Mr Pearson's taking his usual place, at last. Meggie glances towards her own class.

'You better go,' I tell her.

'See you later, Mikey,' she says, and she's gone.

I've still got Steffi and Julie with me, and now Tina's joined them; none of the boys, though. Mr Pearson looks us over in that Roman emperor kind of a way, then raises an arm. I'll say one thing for him. He's pompous but he can get the school quiet, even out here with traffic rumbling past the front gate. He peers at us through his heavy glasses and the buzz of talk stops.

'I'm very pleased with the way you all responded to the fire drill,' he booms, 'much better than last time. Your teachers will now take you back to your lessons, starting with Mr Prescott's group and working from the left.'

I keep to the back when it comes to our turn and let Steffi, Julie and Tina get ahead. They haven't lost interest in me—I get the impression other people are watching too—so I've got to be careful and quick. I might only get one chance, but if it comes, I've got to grab it. Because I can't take any more of this. I don't even want Meggie checking how I am, and she's bound to be looking for me again on our way back to lessons. I let the others get further ahead, make like I'm still following, then wait, wait, wait, and go.

Down the quadrangle, down the steps by the gym, through the door and out towards the bike sheds. The daylight tears into me at once but I've been bracing myself all the way from the quadrangle and I keep on running. Nobody here, not yet, hopefully not at all. No playground to tempt them, thank God, just the school allotments and—at the far end—the groundsman's lodge. I check for Mr Gregory. No sign of him, but he could be anywhere. The daylight's getting sharper, fiercer, more angry—and bloody dark again. I never understand how light can be dark, but never the darkness I want. It goes on cutting into me.

But here's the groundsman's lodge. I glance in at the little window, hoping Mr Gregory's not here. He isn't. Round the back to his shed, check again, the light now screaming inside my head. I see the little field, the wall that marks the perimeter of the school grounds—nothing and nobody, whoopee. I fumble at the door of the shed, praying it's not locked. It hardly ever is and it mustn't be now. It opens like an old friend. I dive inside and close it after me.

'Jesus bloody Christ.'

My voice sounds like it belongs to someone else, someone demented. I lean back against the door, my eyes closed. I can feel my breath jerking in and out. It's some time before it settles and even then I keep my eyes closed. Then I open them and stare round the dusky shed. I love this place, specially as it's got no windows, but I don't often get the chance to escape here. If Mr Gregory's around, or someone else, I can't risk it. Once someone sees me coming here, or coming back out of it, I won't be able to use it again.

I check round the shed. It's not dark inside but it's nice and dim and I don't have to duck the screaming brightness echoing through my eyes and into my head. Nothing much seems to have moved since the last time I came here. Can't remember when that was. Couple of weeks ago, I think. It's not often possible to get here without someone seeing where I'm going. Mr Gregory's usually somewhere near, though he's never barged in on me yet. In fact, I've never actually seen him use this place.

And maybe he doesn't. Maybe that's why the hoes and rakes and spades are stacked like they were last time. Everybody in my class knows Mr Gregory drinks, and that's probably why he disappears inside the groundsman's lodge for so long. But even when he's disappeared, there's usually other people around who could see me, so I have to be careful. Nobody now, though, thank God. I slump to the floor and lean back against the wall. Then the door opens.

And it's them.

CHAPTER 9

They look different from when I saw them watching me over the wall, or the other day. Maybe it's just the russet of the beech trees behind them where the fence cuts the school land from the open field beyond. But what does that matter? It's him and it's her. I'm just praying the rest aren't hanging around nearby. They don't talk. They just stare down at me like I'm scum. Only there's something else in their eyes too. I'm not just scum. I'm posh scum. Even with my uniform as messy as it is, I'm posh to them.

Their clothes couldn't be more different from mine. No uniform for starters—got no idea if they go to a school near the place I saw them the other day—and what they're wearing looks like cast-offs, the things a charity shop would throw away because it's too rough to sell. They're older than me. I'm guessing he's seventeen, she's about the same, but it makes no difference. I'm toast, however old or young they are; and now they've had a good look at me, they're ready to move things on. The guy leans close.

'You was supposed to ring, posh boy.'

His long, dirty hair flicks round his face as he talks. At least the girl looks like she washes occasionally. But her eyes are as hard as his and her lip piercings make her look even fiercer. The guy speaks again, sharply.

'We got questions for you, so you better come with us.'

'I'm not going anywhere,' I mutter.

'Going to have to make him,' says the girl.

The guy moves so fast it throws me. I was expecting him to say something back to the girl, but his hand just shoots out and I feel his fingers scrunch round the collar of my blazer.

'Nice uniform,' he murmurs. 'Cost a lot, did it?'

'Let go.'

'Get up!'

I don't move. He's going to have to pick me up and carry me. He grabs my hair, squeezes it till I yelp, pulls my face round.

'Like that, do you, posh boy?'

He grabs one of the garden forks, turns it so the prongs are pointing at me.

'No!' I say.

I try to twist my face away but he squeezes my hair tighter, locks my head still, and now the girl's got her hands over my cheeks, holding me firm. I squeeze my eyes shut. The girl's fingers force them open again, and there's the prong edging closer, like a huge metal spit. The guy laughs.

'Having fun, posh boy?'

'Don't!'

The prong stops moving, but stays where it is, blocking even the daylight screaming through the open door. The guy whispers into my ear.

'I told you, posh boy,' he says, 'we got questions, so are you coming? Or do I got to stab your eye out first?'

'I'll come.'

'Thought you might.'

He throws the fork to the side and they yank me to my feet. I don't resist. There's no point, and anyway, I've got something new to worry about. The daylight already feels more scary now I'm standing up, and it gets worse as they pull me towards the door. I turn my head, catch a stream of images from the inside of the shed: nothing clear, just the memory of rakes, hoes, the discarded fork, the darkness I came looking for. But the light's caught me first. The russet of the beech trees has faded. Maybe the brightness has swallowed it, or I'm just not seeing any more.

I glance at the guy and the girl. It's hard to make them out now that the light's drowning everything, but they're still just visible. I know they're going to kill me. That stuff about wanting to talk's just a bluff. They want me dead. They must do, after what happened. I just wonder if they know how scared I'd still be if they weren't here, how much more dangerous than them the light feels. The girl's watching me quizzically, like she's picked up some of this. I stare back at her and see what looks like a frown creep over her face, then she turns to her mate.

'Let's get him out of here,' she says.

They shove me out of the door and I stumble into the light. The brightness pours into my eyes like a blinding stream, filling my head with its poison glow; and then it darkens, as the terror opens me up inside. Something claps over my head, something dark in another way: my blazer. They've ripped it off and flung it over me. They'll never know how grateful I am for it, even though they're leading me to my death.

I'm stooping low. Someone's hand's pushing me downwards—the girl's, I think—but I'm stumbling forward somehow, in the direction they want me to go: the beech trees, I'm sure of it, even with my eyes closed tight. I try to remember the colour, the beautiful russet of the foliage, but it won't stay in my head. The terror's eating everything, even what's waiting for me beyond the fence.

We're almost there. I still haven't tripped over, even pushed down like this. I think of my school bag suddenly. Don't know why. Just hits me all at once that I don't know where it is. Can't remember if I brought it with me to the shed or dropped it or left it somewhere else. What the hell am I thinking about that for? But I want to hold it. Maybe I just want to cling on to something: my books inside, the copy of *Moby Dick* that I brought with me today, to help me get through things, but the memory fades, and suddenly it's as if there won't ever be any more books, any more anything.

Even Meggie.

I'm mumbling her name, as they shove me along, but then the pushing stops, and I'm standing there, swaying, bent over, the hand still there. It's clutching the collar of my shirt, keeping control, but it doesn't need to. I'm not going anywhere. They can finish what they came to do. I'm never going to stop them. The hand gives a tug, and another hand nudges me in the back, and I'm moving forward again.

Something hard digs into my side. I stop but the hands move me on. The hard thing scrapes my shirt, but then I'm past it, and I know where I am now: through the fence, the beech trees behind me, and here's the slope under my feet and I'm heading down, towards the brook. OK, I get it. I know how they're going to do it now. Sweet and simple, no fuss, and sure enough, I hear the voices of the others ahead.

Waiting to kill me.

CHAPTER 10

I open my eyes, under the blazer. I'm still murmuring Meggie's name. Don't know if they can hear it. I don't want them to. But I can't stop. I've got to say her name. I want her to be the last thing I remember, the last word I speak. I stare at the ground. Even here, with my head covered, I can feel the brightness tearing into me, but it's bearable, just. I'm praying they won't tear off the blazer too soon. Then off it comes, in one go.

'Ah!'

I can't help the scream. Someone grabs me by the throat and throws me to the ground. I tumble on to the bank of the brook and start to roll down towards the water. A tree root stops me. I twist my head away from the sky, close my eyes as tight as they'll go. A hand seizes me by the hair, yanks my face round, and there's the fingers again, moving over my cheeks like they did before. I recognize the feel of them, the hard menace. They belong to the girl with the lip piercings. She forces my eyes open, like she did before.

The light drives into me again and I squirm, trying to hold back another scream, but I'm moaning badly, wriggling about, aware of the shadows craning over me. Can't see any faces, can't even count how many there are. I can guess the two who sat on the wall, and caught me, and bundled me here. The girl's closest, the guy to her right, but I'm not sure about the others. The light's so bright now, it's blinded me to everything. One thing I am sure about, though. The person I remember most isn't here. No question. Because that's the one person I've been searching for.

'Just do it,' I murmur.

Someone answers, a guy.

'Do what, posh boy?'

'Drown me.'

'Drown you?' he says in mock surprise. 'But we just want to talk, posh boy. We want to ask you some questions. All you gotta do is give us the right answers.'

It won't be that simple. It can't be. The brightness goes on pouring into me. I'm gone now. They can't talk to me and they can't hurt me any more, even if they want to, because there's nothing left to hurt.

'Meggie!' I yell.

Can't hold it back. Got to scream her name to the sky in case I don't get another chance. I scream it again, and in the silence that follows I hear the sound of the dog. It's not a bark, just the familiar scamper of paws and staccato breaths, growing rapidly louder, and then suddenly he's among us, Mr Gregory's pride and joy, the monster mongrel I've always hated but never loved so much as I do now. He's snarling and snapping around us, his idea of fun, and already I can feel the figures moving away. But they call to me as they go.

'We ain't finished talking, posh boy.'

'We got questions and we want answers.'

'Don't talk to nobody else.'

'Or people gonna end up dead.'

'Including you, man.'

'So keep your mouth shut. You got that?'

The dog starts growling, still in fun.

'I don't think they like you, Scabby,' I murmur.

I'm right. Even blinded like this, I can tell that the gang have gone. The mongrel's barking fiercely now, as though he thinks the more noise he makes, the more they'll like him and come back, but they don't, and a moment later I catch Mr Gregory's slurred voice, as harsh and unpleasant a sound as his dog, and every bit as welcome.

'Scab! Where you gone, boy?'

The dog stays close to me and goes on barking. I stand up, shakily. The sky now feels like molten light pouring through my head, through my brain, down inside my neck and into my body. I jam my hands over my eyes, duck my head, feel the drippy nose of the mongrel push against my trousers, then catch Mr Gregory's voice again.

'Molyneux! What are you doing down there?'

And then—unbelievably—Meggie's voice.

'Mikey!'

I don't know how she does this. She always seems to sense when I'm in trouble, and where to find me. But I didn't expect her this time. I thought this was it. I turn in the direction of her voice, but all I hear is Mr Gregory's again, somewhere in the blinding light.

'Stay there, Molyneux! Don't move!'

As if I bloody could. Doesn't he know I'm rooted like a tree? I feel his shadow loom through the brightness. His face and body are blurred and I'm glad I heard his voice first or I'd have thought the gang had come back. I search the light for Meggie's shadow—it won't be far away now—and there it is. She speaks quickly, as if to reassure me.

'It's me, Mikey,' she says, and then, 'Get down, Scab.'

The dog's quietened a bit, but Mr Gregory's now roaring at me.

'What's happened, boy? Look me in the face!'

'He can't,' says Meggie.

'Why not?'

'He's having a panic attack.'

'That's not a panic attack,' says the groundsman. 'I had one myself last year. Wasn't anything like this. I was just lying on my bed and I started hyperventilating. Doctor told me later I'd had a panic attack. That's nothing like your brother. Look at him. He's bent over with his hands over his eyes and—'

'Can we get him indoors, Mr Gregory?'

'He's best out here. Fresh air to calm him down.'

Stupid bastard, but Meggie takes no notice, just takes my hand, slips her other arm round my waist, and guides me up the slope. The dog's nuzzling my leg again as he follows us, and I feel Mr Gregory lumbering along too. Meggie keeps hold of me, murmuring as we go.

'Come on, big guy.'

We reach the top, and the brightness starts to ease. It still feels dangerous, and ready to attack again, but being with Meggie's making the difference and I plod on with half-open eyes. Ahead of us is the shed with the door flung back, and I can make out the rakes and hoes and the discarded fork, and my school bag, thrust in the corner.

'Meggie?' I murmur.

'Yeah, big guy?'

'How did you know where I was?'

'I found your bag.'

'How did you do that?'

'Lucky guess.'

No, it wasn't. You can't be lucky as often as she is. She just knows where I am, and when I need her most. I love you, I tell her in my head, I love you so much. But she knows that too, even when I don't tell her properly.

'I love you, big guy,' she says. 'OK, stay here while I get your bag out of the shed.'

I don't want her to let go, but I know she's got to. She leaves me and runs over to the shed. I stand there, swaying again, feeling like I'm going to fall. A hand catches me, a different hand: heavy, gnarly. I peer round into Mr Gregory's face. It's clear, in spite of the glare, and he's stuck his head close. I've got his bloodshot eyes glowering into me, though they probably mean no harm. Can't say the same for his breath, though. I turn away.

'I'm not going to fall over,' I tell him.

His hand stays on me. I want to prise it off, but luckily Meggie's back now, and she takes charge again like she always does, even with adults.

'I'll get Michael back into school, Mr Gregory.'

'I'll come with you,' he mutters.

'It's all right, sir, I can do it. I'm used to these attacks.

56

I'll take him straight to the nurse, then tell Mr Cable. Thank you so much for helping him.'

Mr Gregory grunts, but eventually lets go, and Meggie steers me towards the main building. The dog follows, nuzzling my legs as before. Mr Gregory bellows at him from behind us.

'Scab! Come back!'

The dog takes no notice.

'Scab!'

Meggie stops—one hand holding my arm, the other my bag—and looks down at the dog.

'Back you go, Scab,' she says quietly.

And the dog turns and runs back towards Mr Gregory. Meggie glances at me again.

'Let's get you safe, Mikey,' she says.

CHAPTER 11

She doesn't take me to the nurse, or to Mr Cable, but she does get me safe. Back into the main building and away from the daylight, then right down the corridor and right again to the little alcove outside the drama room. Nobody here but I catch voices beyond the door, Mrs Janner calling everyone together, and now they're improvising a theft in a shop or something. I'm not really listening. Meggie eases me into the corner by the coats hanging on the pegs, sits me down on the bench, looks into my face.

'What happened out there, big guy?' she says.

I glance towards the drama room door. Meggie speaks again.

'They can't hear us, Mikey.'

But she's lowered her voice. I look back at her, lower mine too.

'Usual thing,' I say.

'What do you mean?'

'Being me, being outside.'

'But you didn't have to go outside,' she says. 'What were you doing by the brook?'

'What were *you* doing by the brook?' I say. 'You're supposed to be in Science.'

'Don't change the subject, Mikey.'

'I didn't mean to go to the brook,' I say. 'I went to Mr Gregory's shed. I was in there.'

'What for?'

'It's the closest place I know to the wardrobe.'

Meggie frowns.

'So why the brook?' she says.

'I heard Mr Gregory coming and ran off. I couldn't go back to the main building or he'd have seen me.'

'You could have cut left round the back of the gardens and gone in that way. He'd never have seen you, specially in his state.'

'I panicked.'

She's watching me with a sad look. I've seen it before. Whenever she knows I'm lying to her.

'What really happened, Mikey?' she says. 'Tell me.'

I can't, I just can't, because if I tell her this, I've got to tell her about the gang, and everything else, and she mustn't know, nobody must. *Talk to anyone else and people gonna die. Including you.* Well, I don't care about me, but I do care about Meggie. I think of the figures by the brook, burning with danger.

'I told you,' I say. 'I panicked. I just blundered out of the shed. Didn't think where I was going.'

Still the sad look. I hate disappointing her.

'Do you want me to get you home, Mikey?'

'I'll ring Mum,' I say. 'You don't have to do it.'

I pull out my mobile. It pings as I do so.

'You've got a text,' says Meggie.

I keep my eyes on her face.

'It'll only be Nip,' I say, 'wondering why I'm not in English.'

It won't be Nip. It'll be them. I know it already. They'll have my mobile number the same way they got my email address. They'll know where I live too. No question.

'Aren't you going to check it?' says Meggie.

'I'll ring Mum first.'

'I'll do it, Mikey. You read your text.'

She pulls out her phone and I look away, feeling guilty. Meggie's soon talking to Mum, quiet, no fuss, nothing critical. Mikey's fine, he's absolutely fine, maybe struggling just a bit, think he'll be better at home today. Can you come in and get him? OK, see you at Reception.

It's like they're talking in a code they've worked out between themselves. Don't know why I'm noticing it now. It's been there as long as I can remember. Dad speaks it too, fluently, and suddenly I'm wondering what they say about me when it's just the three of them and they don't need the code. The guilt stays, deepens. I hear Meggie's voice again.

'Mikey, let's go.'

We stand up. Least she's forgotten about the text.

'You didn't check your text,' she says.

I walk off without answering. Meggie catches me up. Doesn't say anything but I feel her eyes glance at my mobile. I push it into my pocket, then realize with another stab of guilt that she's still carrying my bag.

'Give me that,' I say.

She lets me take it, hooks her hand inside my arm, then unhooks it again. I see Marco and Ben from my form group heading towards us. They walk past without a word, checking Meggie as they go. She waits till they're out of sight, then takes my arm again.

'What was that about?' I say.

'What do you mean, Mikey?'

'Embarrassed to be seen holding my arm?'

She pulls me to a halt, her eyes flashing.

'I was thinking the opposite, you idiot, thinking you'd be the one feeling embarrassed. Your little sister holding on to you in front of your mates. Christ, Mikey!'

Another stab of guilt, yet another. I want to say sorry but all I can do is drop my eyes and mumble.

'They're not my mates.'

She starts to walk on but I catch her arm.

'Meggie, sorry.'

She looks at me, still hurt.

'I know I'm a basket case,' I say.

She doesn't contradict me. I hesitate.

'I don't want everything to revolve round me.'

'It doesn't,' she says quietly.

'OK.'

'But we care about you, Mikey. You matter.'

'You matter too, Meggie.'

My mobile pings again. Meggie glances towards my pocket, then moves off without a word. I catch her up. She gives me a smile but we stay quiet and walk on, the corridors empty, just a murmur of voices in classrooms as we pass. She turns down the east quadrangle, a roundabout route to Reception but the way I'd have gone if I'd been on my own: the darkest way. I love her for knowing this. She gives me another smile, like

61

she's just picked this up. I think of the courage she's got and I haven't. I hate letting her down. I know I've got to do better for her, got to be braver, not just about going out of doors, but about everything. If Meggie had my stuff, she'd just deal with it. So I've got to deal with it too.

'What you thinking, big guy?' she says.

'You probably know already.'

'I'm not a mind-reader, Mikey.'

She is, she absolutely is. I reckon fifty per cent of the time she knows what's in my head. I just hope the fifty she doesn't pick up is the bit I've got to keep from her.

'Come on, Mikey,' she says, 'what's buzzing your brain?'

'I was just thinking I hate letting you down.'

She doesn't answer straight away, just walks slowly on, then suddenly she looks at me.

'You don't let me down, Mikey,' she says. 'I'm proud of you. I love being your sister.'

'Meggie—'

'And Mum and Dad are proud of you too. They really are.'

'I'm such a coward.'

'You're not a coward,' she says. 'We all know it's hard for you. Mikey, listen.'

I know what's coming—even I can mind-read this bit—and I know what I've got to say back to her. If I'm ever going to make her believe in me.

'Let's go back to that place we went to,' she says, 'just you and me. You managed it before, Mikey. I know you got upset on the way back but that's just because you hadn't ever been there. It'll be easier next time. What do you think?'

My mobile pings again. Meggie's eyes flick towards my pocket but I keep mine on her face.

'Sure,' I say. 'Let's do it.'

CHAPTER 12

I sit at Reception with Mrs Warby. Meggie's left me and gone back to Science. I thought I'd have to persuade her to go but it seems there's more code going on and everybody who matters is in on it, everybody except me, that is. A squeeze of my hand and Meggie's gone, and Mrs Warby tells me Mum's already phoned in to say she's on her way, and somebody's told Mr Cable I'm going home, and somebody else has sent a message to Mr Hart in Science to explain Meggie's absence.

So everybody's on top of things—only I'm sitting here staring through the big glass doors into the school car park and thinking and frowning and feeling more guilt, and trying to find a reason not to check my mobile. But it's no good, there isn't one, and anyway, I'm supposed to be working on courage. I pull the thing out. Three identical texts stare up at me: no sender's name, just the message:

Keep your mouth shut mikey or people gonna die now ring this number xxx

I stare at it. Not a local number. A mobile number, and not the one that sent these texts. I feel Mrs Warby move nearby. She was sitting behind her desk a moment ago but she's coming over to see me. I push the mobile back in my pocket.

'Do you want something to drink, Michael?' she says.

'No, thanks.'

And I don't want to talk either, even to nice people like Mrs Warby. I just want to think. She gives me a pat on the shoulder.

'Your mother will be here soon.'

She's here now. I've just seen her driving in through the school gates and now she's looking for a parking spot. But I'm not really watching her. I'm watching two figures hunched on a motorbike out in the street. Don't know who they are but they've stopped by the entrance and they're staring in Mum's direction as she backs into a slot by the school minibuses.

Wish she'd parked a bit nearer to the main door. The daylight looks like it could cut through me. But maybe it's best like this. If I'm really going to fight back, I've got to start braving it more. I think of Meggie again, and what she'd do if she were me, and stand up. Mrs Warby gives me another pat.

'There's your mother. What did I tell you?'

I look for the motorbike and see that it's gone.

'Thanks very much, Mrs Warby,' I say.

'No problem at all, Michael.'

I head for the doors, Mrs Warby walking with me. I want her to go back so I can meet Mum by myself, but that's clearly not the plan; and now Mum's inside the building, and the two women have greeted each other, and the code's begun again. They're talking about the weather, the traffic, the new one-way system, but I'm not stupid: I know I'm the subject, I know the code's still there, even if I can't understand it. But we're moving off at last. A nod from Mrs Warby and then I'm outside with Mum.

'How do you want to do this, Mikey?' she says. 'I could bring the car closer to the steps or give you the keys and you can run ahead and get in by yourself.'

I think of Meggie again, and what she'd do.

'I'll walk with you to the car, Mum.'

'OK.'

She doesn't believe me. I can hear it in her voice. But I don't blame her. I almost always dash from one closed space to another. I stare at the car. I hate its wide, shiny windows but it's got a roof, which is better than nothing. Only I've got to walk there. I can't sprint like I usually do, or this won't count.

'Let's go, Mum.'

She doesn't move. She's watching and I know why. She wants to see if I'll charge off, bent over, eyes to the ground. I set off down the steps, slow as I can. She catches me up.

'Keep going, Mikey.'

But it's no good. The light's already pouring over me and, as I feared, it's cutting, cutting, cutting. I want to stop, dip my head, screw my eyes shut, turn, and duck back inside the school building. I keep going somehow but my body's shuddering. I fix my eyes on the steps. We're at the bottom now, and Mum's caught me by the arm and she's steering me in the direction of the car. I can't have her do this. I've got to manage by myself.

I ease Mum's hand from my arm. The shuddering grows worse, the light more vicious. I break into a run. Mum calls after me.

'Mikey!'

I stop, my eyes straining to close. I keep them open somehow, but all I want to do is die. I think of Meggie again, her beautiful strength. I whisper to her.

'Meggie.'

Mum speaks, close to my ear.

'Mikey?'

Her face is a cloud of flame, no features at all. I speak again to Meggie inside my head.

What do I do?

The words come straight back.

Pretend you love the light.

I turn in the direction of the car and walk on, Mum's hand on my arm again. I don't brush it away this time. I'm not bothered about the hand now. I feel Meggie's with me. Don't care if I'm imagining it. All I know is the car's getting nearer and I'll settle for that. Mum seems to settle for it too. She's murmuring encouragement as we walk. We reach the car and she speaks again.

'Do you want to go in the back, Mikey?'

She's waiting for me to say yes, to dive in like I usually do and shove my head down the back of the driver's seat as close to the floor as it'll go. I think of Meggie again.

'I'll sit in the front, Mum.'

'OK.'

Wasn't expecting her to say that. I was thinking and half-hoping she'd try to chivvy me into the back. I feel a moment of panic. I hate the front seats, but I guess there's always the dashboard. I could bend down and stick my head under that if things get bad. But even as I think this, I hear Meggie's voice inside me again.

You don't need the dashboard.

I climb into the front of the car, close the door, clip on the safety belt. Mum climbs in the other side, the brightness swirling around her. Meggie's voice comes back.

Pretend you love the light.

'I'll try,' I mutter

I feel Mum's hand again.

'You're mumbling things, Mikey,' she says. 'You were doing it before.'

'Can we go home, please?'

'Of course.'

She starts the engine and we drive out of the school gates into the queue of cars crawling towards the roundabout.

'Traffic's terrible today, Mikey,' Mum says, 'as I was saying to Mrs Warby.'

We move, stop, move, stop, move, stop; and that's when I hear the motorbike.

CHAPTER 13

I see it a moment later. It's in the wing mirror and, even with the brightness pushing into my eyes, I make out the shape: a dark image, looming, and then it stops. I hear the engine rev up, see the figures, but not the faces: the visors are down, both tinted. I sense it's teenagers: something about the posture. They've driven up the inside, cutting between stationary cars, and they could easily ride past if they wanted to, but they don't. They just sit there, level with the boot of our car, the engine still revving. I see the gloved hand working the throttle.

'Why does he have to keep doing that?' says Mum, watching too. 'I'm sure it can't be good for the engine. And why doesn't he ride on? He's got a clear run to the roundabout. I wish we had. Ah, at last.'

The cars in front are edging forward. Mum follows, peering ahead. I keep my eyes on the wing mirror. The motorbike's moving too but only to stay level with our boot.

'Damn,' says Mum.

The cars in front are stopping again. She brings us to a halt and pulls up the handbrake, then glances back again.

'What is it with that bike?' she says. 'They're just sitting there.'

They're not. They're creeping forward, super-slow, super-quiet, no heavy throttle this time, just a chilly darkness filling the wing mirror, and now they're alongside. Neither head's turning my way, but I'm watching them closely, and Mum is too.

'Least he's stopped revving the thing up,' she says.

I don't answer. I'm watching for a swinging arm with a hammer or a brick, but there's nothing from either of them, not even a glance. Then a hand moves. It's not from the rider but the guy on the back: he's pulling off a glove, and now the other one, and stuffing them in a pocket, and something's coming out, a mobile, and he's punching something in—and I know what's going to happen next. The motorbike hovers, level with the wing mirror, and my mobile pings with a text.

'Yours, Mikey,' says Mum.

I ignore it.

'Yours,' she says.

'It's only a text, Mum. I'll read it later.'

'That's not like you.'

I shrug, say nothing.

'Might be Meggie,' says Mum.

I see the rider working the throttle again. The engine starts squealing.

'It's getting really annoying,' says Mum, 'that biker making so much din.'

I reach into my pocket for the mobile, pull it out, check the message.

Ring mikey say nothing to nobody and ring we gotta talk

I see the helmets twist as the figures turn to watch me, visors still down. I think of Meggie again and words rush into my head. *Pretend you're brave even if you're not.* I turn towards the bikers and give them a V-sign.

'Mikey!' says Mum. 'I saw that. What are you doing?'

I don't answer, don't look at her. I'm watching the guy on the back of the bike. No movement at first, and for a moment I wonder if he somehow missed the gesture, then he pushes the visor up and I get his eyes glaring down at me: they're hard, bullety things—and then suddenly they're gone, because the bike's powered off.

'Thank God for that,' says Mum, staring after them.

I watch the bike shoot past the front of the queue, skin the roundabout, and disappear down Melton Lane. Mum turns quickly back to me.

'What were you thinking of, Mikey?' she says.

'I don't know.'

'That was crazy. Was it bravado?'

'I suppose so.'

'Well, it was a silly thing to do,' she says, 'especially to people as aggressive as that. We could have had a really nasty incident. Don't ever do that again, Mikey, even if you feel provoked.'

I switch off my mobile and we sit in silence for a while, then, to my relief, the traffic clears and we eventually make it home. A minute later I'm in my wardrobe with the door firmly closed. It doesn't help much and I don't suppose it ever will. I'm not stupid. I know it's me running away, or trying to, rather than facing up, fronting up, or whatever people want to call it. I know what

Mr Braine calls it: taking ownership of your fear, which sounds good, I suppose, until you realize it's bollocks.

But the wardrobe's still my first go-to place at times like this, long as I can get in without too much fuss from Mum and Dad. Normally they turn a blind eye to it. They make out it's not happening and only get involved when I stay in there too long and have to be coaxed out. Not Meggie, though. She takes me on before I even get in there, like she's feeling the ache in my heart.

'Don't go in the wardrobe, big guy,' she'll say, and then tweak my cuff and give me that smile. 'You don't need to hide in there.'

What can you do with a sister like that? But Meggie's not here right now, and Mum's clattering about the kitchen, pretending she doesn't know I'm in here, so I've got some time to myself. I pull out my phone, switch it on, and read the last text again. As I do so, a new one comes in.

We dont like what you done mikey bad move

I think back to the motorbike. Mum was right. It was stupid giving them the V-sign. It was just the same sort of boneheaded bravado as when I told Meggie where I wanted to go the other night and insisted I was cool about it when I knew deep down I wasn't. Big, big mistake, not just because of the kind of place it is, but because of what happened there and what's happened since. All because of bravado. And yet . . .

I keep thinking about bravery. Is that the same as bravado or is it something different? I don't know. All I'm certain about is that I'm letting Meggie down every time I act the wimp. I think of those words. I'm sure I heard them in my head, even with Meggie's beautiful voice. *Pretend you're brave even if you're not.* I look down at the text message, read the number they've given me. I can't do this. I can't ring them, even for Meggie. The phone pings with another text.

Ring ring ring

I think of Meggie again, wish she was here with me, sitting in the darkness—and suddenly she is, in the darkness of my head, her voice clear and strong.

You can do it, big guy.

I ring the number, trembling.

CHAPTER 14

I want to hang up again before anyone answers but I've got Meggie's voice hammering away and it's like she's telling me I'll be more scared if I don't see this through. I think she's wrong, but I stay on the line, praying no one'll answer. Someone does, only there's no voice, no breathing, no background noise, just silence: then, after a moment, a low, mocking laugh. I hear Mum coming up the stairs. Silence falls again at the other end of the phone. Mum stops outside the room, then knocks on my bedroom door. I don't answer. She opens it and calls through.

'Mikey?'

I hear another laugh at the other end of the phone. Mum calls again, more loudly.

'Mikey, please come out of the wardrobe.'

I hang up and push the phone back in my pocket. As I do so, it pings with another text. I reach in and switch it off. Mum taps on the wardrobe door.

'Mikey, please come out of there.'

Again I hear Meggie's voice inside my head.

Move your arse, big guy. You don't have to hide in there.

I lunge for the wardrobe door, but it opens ahead of me, and I see Mum's face.

'I was just coming out,' I tell her.

She doesn't look convinced, but I don't blame her for that. I don't normally give in this easily. She's holding *Treasure Island*, but keeping it just out of reach, as Meggie did with *Moby Dick* this morning.

'Couldn't you find a carrot?' I mutter.

I know it's a cheap remark. Mum looks puzzled and I don't think she got it. Maybe it's just as well. I shouldn't be horrible to Mum when she's being nice and I'm being a pain, and now, just to make me feel even more guilty, she holds the book out. Part of me wants to take it, ask her to hand me my torch as well, then curl up inside the wardrobe and stay here for another few hours, but that would be a horrible thing to do to her, and anyway, Meggie's letting rip inside my head.

Move your arse, big guy! What's wrong with you?

I ignore the book and scramble out of the wardrobe. Mum ruffles my hair.

'Well done, darling.'

'I love you, Mum,' I say quickly, 'just so you know.'

'I love you too, Mikey. Don't you want the book?'

I take it from her and put it back on the shelf in its usual place. Mum smiles at me, then sits down on the edge of the desk and glances round the room.

'Sorry about the mess,' I say.

'I was just thinking how tidy everything is.' She looks back at me. 'Mikey, you still haven't told me about today.'

'Not much to tell.'

'Tell me anyway.'

'I just got confused,' I say. 'That's all. You know what I'm like.'

'Meggie said you were hiding in the groundsman's shed.'

I stare at her.

'Meggie never told you that.'

'She did, Mikey.'

'No, she didn't. I heard her talking to you on the phone and she never mentioned the shed.'

'Easy, Mikey,' says Mum 'She texted me about it a few minutes ago. While you were up here.'

I scowl at her. Feels wrong somehow: Meggie texting Mum about the shed. Don't know why I think that. I suppose I just expected her to keep it secret. I certainly wanted her to. Mum pulls out her mobile and offers it to me.

'Read Meggie's text, Mikey.'

'It's none of my business.'

'Read it.'

I look away. Mum reads it aloud.

'Mum, can you keep an eye on Mikey? He's really, really frightened about something at the moment and I'm worried about him. I found him by the brook. He'd been hiding in the groundsman's shed. Stay close to him till I get home.'

I feel another wave of guilt.

'She's looking out for you, Mikey.'

'I know,' I say, 'like you.'

'And Dad.'

'I know. I'm sorry I'm such a wimp.'

'You're not a wimp, Mikey, but what's this about the groundsman's shed? And the brook?'

76

I look back at her. I've got pictures flooding me, not just of the shed and the brook, but of what happened the other night, what Meggie didn't see and mustn't know, what nobody must know. The gang can't just want to talk. They're too dangerous and I know too much, and this isn't just about them and me. It's about other people, people I care about. *Talk to anyone else and people gonna die.* I can't let that happen. I look at Mum. She's wanting to talk too. She's watching me with that look that says 'I'm not moving till you answer my questions'.

'I just panicked,' I tell her. 'I went and hid in Mr Gregory's shed. Then I wandered down to the brook.'

'Wandered?'

'Blundered.'

'Why the shed?'

'You know why.'

'Because it's dark in there?'

'Yes.'

'So why go outside again?' she says. 'Why go down to the brook?'

'I told you. I panicked.'

Mum looks at me, frowning.

'Meggie says you're frightened about something at the moment. Is she right?'

'You know me, Mum.'

'Is she right, Mikey?'

I shrug.

'I'm always nervy about stuff. Nothing new about that.'

'Meggie didn't say you're nervy about stuff,' says Mum. 'She said you're frightened about something, which I take to mean something in particular, not just the usual things you find difficult.' Mum checks the text again. 'Really, really frightened about something, she says. Meggie's exact words. What's going on, Mikey?'

I look down.

'Nothing.'

'Mikey, look at me.'

I meet Mum's eyes again.

'What's going on, Mikey? Tell me.'

I hold her gaze as well as I can.

'Nothing, Mum. I promise.'

The moment she's gone I switch on my mobile again. No surprise who sent the text. I can almost hear the guy's mocking laugh as I read the words.

Come out the wardrobe mikey

Shit, he heard Mum calling to me. I feared he must have done. Another text comes in, same leery bastard.

Stay in the wardrobe mikey and you gonna die in the wardrobe

Ping! Another text.

Talk to us mikey talky talky

Ping!

Talk to us and live mikey.

Ping!

Talk to anyone else and people gonna die

Ping!

Including you mikey xxx

I think of Meggie, feel her strength, press Reply, type the words:

Piss off piss off piss off

Then cancel the text. Meggie's voice comes raging into my head.

Type it again, big guy, and this time send it!

'You piss off too, Meggie,' I mutter, but I don't mean it of course. I can't believe I'm talking aloud to an empty room. I pull down *Treasure Island* and stroke it.

'Sorry, Meggie,' I murmur. 'I don't want you to piss off.'

Stand up for yourself, big guy.

'I'm not like you, Meggie. I wish I was but I'm not.'

The phone rings. I squeeze *Treasure Island*; check the mobile. No name showing, just a new number I don't recognize. I stare at it. I'm not answering this. I'm bloody not. I let it go on ringing. I hear Meggie loud in my head. *Answer the phone, Mikey!* I answer the phone and hear Meggie's voice again.

'What happened to you, big guy?'

Only this time it's really her.

CHAPTER 15

'Not answering your phone, Mikey?' she says.

I push *Treasure Island* against my cheek, hold it tight.

'You there, Mikey?'

'Yeah.'

'Thought you weren't going to answer,' she says. 'You let it ring for ages.'

'What happened to your phone? This isn't your number.'

'Battery's run down,' she says. 'Stupid me.'

'So whose phone are you using?'

'Ringo's.'

'Ringo's?'

'Get off!' she says suddenly.

But it's not to me. It's to someone else, someone with her. I listen hard but all I hear is chatter and laughter further off. Nobody I recognize. I call into the phone.

'Meggie?'

No answer, then, 'Get off!' she says again.

More chatter, more laughter. It's definitely boys. Then suddenly she's back.

'Mikey, you still there?'

'What's going on, Meggie?'

'Just Ringo mucking about. Mikey, listen—'

'What are you using Ringo's phone for?'

'I told you,' she says. 'I forgot to charge mine up.'

'But why Ringo's?'

'I was going to ask Nip but he's not here. I'll tell you why in a minute.'

'Why didn't you ask Lucy?'

'What?'

'Why didn't you ask Lucy? Or one of your other friends?'

'Because I saw Ringo first,' she says. 'Christ's sake, Mikey, what's up with you?'

'What did you want to ask me?' I say flatly.

'Eh?'

'What did you want to ask me?' I hate the hardness in my voice but I can't help it. Ringo of all people. First, he thinks I'm a wanker, and second, he's all over Meggie. 'You borrowed Ringo's phone. What did you want to ask me?'

There's a silence, even from Ringo and the others, which I suppose means they're all listening. Then Meggie again.

'Hold on, Mikey.'

Another silence, but she's soon back, talking low.

'Listen, Mikey,' she says, 'I've moved away from the guys—'

'The guys?'

'Yeah, the guys,' she says.

'What, are you all buddies now?'

'Mikey, what's got into you?' Meggie's still talking low, if anything quieter than before. 'They're just guys,

81

OK? And I've moved away so I can talk to you properly.'

'So why the low voice?' I say. 'I don't see the point. If there's nobody else around.'

'Bloody hell, Mikey!' She says that loud enough. 'I'll talk to you later, OK?'

'Meggie, don't hang up!'

She doesn't, but I know she wants to.

'Don't hang up, Meggie,' I say. 'Please don't.'

She stays on the line, breathing hard.

'Sorry, Meggie,' I mutter.

'Christ, Mikey,' she says, 'I don't know what gets into you sometimes.'

Her voice has gone quiet again, soft and kind and forgiving. She's let me off much too quickly. As usual.

'I'm a prat, Meggie.'

'Telling me,' she says.

'A big prat.'

'Huge.'

I laugh but she doesn't join in.

'I wish you were here, Meggie,' I say.

I want to tell her I feel she's talking inside my head, but it's probably a bad idea, and she goes on anyway.

'I wish I was there too,' she says, 'but there ought to be at least one Molyneux in school today. Mikey, what's going on? There's something you're not telling me, something really important.'

'No, there isn't.'

'Is it something to do with where we went? You haven't been right since I took you there.'

'I'm fine about it.'

'So you're still up for going back?'

'Sure.'

'Today?' she says. 'When I get home? Cup of tea and straight out again?'

'Yeah.'

'And you promise you'll come?' she says. 'Without any—'

'Mollycoddling, yeah.'

'I wasn't going to say mollycoddling.'

'But you meant that.'

'Maybe.'

'I'll come,' I say. 'I promise.'

She doesn't believe me. She thinks she'll come home, and I'll hide in the wardrobe again and stay there. Trouble is, she's probably right. I feel strong here on the phone, with Meggie at the other end talking to me. It'll be different later with the front door open, and all that horrible space in front of us, and the gang watching our every move. Because they will be. They already are now. I know it. Meggie speaks again suddenly.

'Mikey, listen, I've got to tell you about Nip. He's in a bit of trouble.'

'What kind of trouble?'

'He got into a fight with Russell and hurt him badly. I didn't see it but Ringo and some of the other boys did. Mr Pearson had to get Nip's mum to come in and take him home.'

'Nip never gets into fights.'

'He did this time,' says Meggie, 'and Ringo says Nip started it. He just went for Russell and beat him up. Lost his rag completely, which isn't like Nip. Russell's been taken to hospital.'

'What was the fight about?'

But I already know. I'm just going through the motion of asking.

'It was . . . about you, Mikey,' she says. 'Russell said some stuff about you being—'

'Weird, off my head, creepy, pathetic—'

'Something like that.' Meggie gives a sigh. 'It's nothing you should take seriously, Mikey, OK? People say all kinds of bad things and Russell's always been a prat.'

'I don't care about what Russell said.'

But I do care about Nip. His mum and dad will have gone ballistic. He's only got to get an exam grade that's not as high as they want and he's grounded for a week with his mobile taken away and his internet switched off. The punishment will be even worse for something like this. Meggie speaks again.

'Mikey, listen, I've got go, OK? Ringo wants his phone back.'

I hear Ringo's voice somewhere near her.

'Meggie,' I say, 'has he been standing next to you all this time?'

She doesn't answer. I hear Ringo mumble something, and she turns to the side and mumbles something back. I don't get any of it, apart from one thing.

'He called you babe,' I mutter.

I don't expect an answer, but Meggie gives me one.

'No, he didn't,' she says, 'and no, he hasn't.'

'Hasn't what?'

She lowers her voice yet again.

'He didn't call me babe, and he hasn't been standing next to me all this time. But he is now, Mikey. Well, not

next to me, but nearer, because he wants his phone back,
OK? I'll see you later, Mikey.'

And she's gone. The moment she hangs up, my phone
pings with a text.

Look out your window mikey

I stay where I am, well back.

Ping!

I said look out your window mikey

I realize I'm still holding *Treasure Island*. I stare at it,
then at the mobile.

Ping!

Come on mikey do it

I place the book on the desk and turn to the window. From downstairs comes the sound of Mum in the
kitchen. She's filling the kettle, and now opening the
cupboard with the squeaky door hinge. Now she's rattling cups and saucers. A moment later the radio goes on.
I go on watching the window. I'm not visible from the
street, not yet. I glance at the last message again, try to
imagine the guy's voice speaking the words. Only I get
Meggie's voice instead, thundering inside my head.

Come on, Mikey! Stand up for yourself!

I walk to the window and look out. Nobody in Denbury Close, nobody I can see anyway. Just the same quiet
houses for the same quiet people.

Ping!

Can't see us can you mikey but we can see you.

Ping!

And we want to talk mikey so ring ring ring.

Ping!

But dont tell nobody mikey.

Ping!

Or u no whats gonna happen.

I can still hear the radio downstairs. Mum's got the news on. But Meggie's voice drowns it, and she's only got one message for me. I give her my answer aloud.

'Yeah, I know. Stand up for yourself.'

I press Reply, key in the words.

Go to hell bastards.

Press Send, switch off the phone, walk away.

CHAPTER 16

Mum smiles at me as I enter the kitchen, then reaches over to the radio and turns it off.

'You don't need to do that if you were listening to something,' I say.

'It's only the news, Mikey.'

'So I heard.'

'Doom and gloom.'

She takes me by the hand.

'I've just made some tea.'

'Great.'

'And then, I thought, maybe an omelette?'

'Lovely. Thanks, Mum.'

'Sure?'

'Yeah, great.'

She's watching me warily, like she doesn't know how to talk to me any more or what to say. I hate making her like this, and Dad. He's nervous with me too. Meggie's the only one who doesn't get thrown by me. I think of her strength again, and then the text I just sent. I'm already regretting it. The only thing that makes me feel better is that I know it's what Meggie would want me to do, and she's right: I've got to be braver, got to sort this courage thing out. I can't go on being spineless for the rest of my life. I'll never be as strong as Meggie is, not by miles, but I can try to make her proud of me; and I can try to stop freaking Mum and Dad out too.

'I'd love an omelette, Mum.'

'Good.'

'But only if you're having one too.'

'I'm having one too.'

'And you let me do the cooking.'

'OK,' she says.

I raise an eyebrow.

'You gave in a bit easily there.'

'Did I?' she says.

'You were supposed to insist.'

'Oh.'

'And then tell me to sit down while you do the cooking.'

Mum laughs and hands me the pan. I take it, trying to think of more banter, but I'm not very good at this. Mum seems to have a relaxed a bit, though. She fetches the eggs.

'Can I be chef's assistant?' she says.

'If you play your cards right.'

We make the omelettes together and take them over to the table. I'm starting to fret about the text again but every time I think of it, I get Meggie's voice in my head.

Stand up for yourself, big guy.

Mum's talking as we eat, harmless stuff about Mrs Kennicot's cat pooing in the porch again and old Mr

Blackwell at the corner shop getting more forgetful, easy things that don't need an answer, and I'm managing to nod my head and murmur back. We go on like this, eating and talking, Mum keeping to safe subjects, and it's nice sitting here with her and pretending there's nothing wrong; but then we finish eating and it's like we've finished talking safe too.

'I was wondering about Mr Braine,' says Mum.

'What about him?'

'Whether we should arrange another appointment.'

'What for?'

'You know what for, Mikey. You've been struggling—'

'No more than usual.'

'Much more than usual,' says Mum, 'and now Meggie's saying you've got some particular worry on your mind.'

'I told you that wasn't true.'

'But you're acting as though it's true.'

'Mum—'

'Hear me out, Mikey.' Mum pauses. 'You're acting as though there's some big anxiety in your life, something beyond the usual things that upset you. Dad and I have both noticed it, and now there's Meggie warning us to keep an eye on you. So I'm just wondering whether we ought to get Mr Braine to talk to you again. You haven't seen him for a while—'

'Because it's not working.'

'Because he said you were making progress and you didn't need him so much.' Mum pauses again. 'And you *were* making progress, Mikey, you were doing really well. But you've clearly been finding things tougher recently, so why don't we get Mr Braine to see you again? Just for one session if you like.'

I catch a movement in the window and turn to look. But it's only Mrs Gallagher hobbling past the house.

'Mikey?' says Mum.

I look back at her.

'I don't want to see Mr Braine.'

'Why not?' she says. 'Don't you like him?'

'He talks fancy. I never understand what he's going on about.'

Which isn't exactly true, but it seems a more tactful way of saying he's full of shit. Specially when Mum and Dad have forked out so much money for the treatment.

'You've never told us this before, Mikey,' says Mum.

I'm pretty sure I have but I don't answer. I'm thinking of the text again, and the gang, and Nip. I want to talk to him. Not sure what I want to say apart from thank you. Maybe thank you is all I can say. But I don't suppose his mum and dad will let me close enough to do even that. Mum stands up, takes the empty plates away, and stacks them in the dishwasher. I stand up too.

'Sorry, Mum.'

'No need to say sorry, Mikey. It was just a suggestion about Mr Braine.'

'I meant sorry about everything.'

I hear a car pull up outside the house, a door slam, footsteps on the path, then a key in the front door. A moment later Dad walks in. Mum stares at him.

'What are you doing back?'

'Nice to see you too, darling,' he says.

'I thought you had meetings all afternoon.'

'Meggie rang me and said—'

'Mikey's being a pain,' I say.

Dad turns on me.

'She said Mikey's in a state and he's come home, and that she's worried about you. As we all are.'

I look down.

'Sorry, Dad.'

'Don't make this even harder than it is, Mikey,' he says. 'I know you see the outside world as a kind of enemy, but you mustn't think of your family the same way. We're not the enemy.'

'I know you're not.'

'We're on your side.'

'I know, Dad. I'm sorry. I just . . . say stupid things sometimes.'

Another movement outside the window. Mrs Gallagher again, hobbling back to her house. I watch her till she disappears from view. Mrs Kennicot's cat jumps up on the wall outside our front garden, peers in at me for a moment, then jumps off again. I look back at Dad.

'I'm sorry you came back for me,' I say. 'You didn't need to, specially if you've got meetings.'

'You're more important than meetings, Mikey,' says Dad. He glances at Mum. 'Have you two eaten?'

'We just had omelettes,' says Mum. 'Do you want one?'

'Wouldn't mind,' he says. 'I skipped lunch.'

'I'll make it,' I say.

'I'll do it, Mikey,' says Mum.

Yet another movement outside the window. The cat again, back on the wall. Dad catches sight of it and glowers.

'Bloody thing,' he says to Mum. 'Did you know it shat in our porch again yesterday?'

'Yes, I was telling Mikey.'

He shakes a fist at it. The cat looks on, unimpressed.

'Go away, you bloody—'

'Easy, darling,' says Mum.

But Dad's already striding out of the room. A moment later I hear him outside the house, hissing and clapping his hands. The cat jumps off the wall again, but Dad goes on storming up the street after it. I see Mum watching him, her lips tight together. She looks round at me suddenly, as though she's sensed my eyes on her.

'He'll be all right, Mikey,' she says.

'I hate stressing you both out.'

'You're not stressing us both out.'

She's a hopeless liar, but she goes on trying.

'We're OK, Mikey. Don't worry about us.'

'Look at Dad,' I say. 'You telling me he's OK?'

'He's just concerned about you, and I am too,' she says. 'We wouldn't be very good parents if we weren't a little anxious when we see you going through so much. But we'll cope, Mikey, and we're totally here for you. Don't ever think we're not.'

We turn back to the street. Dad's still out there, but he's given up trying to chase the cat. He's just standing in the middle of the road, staring at nothing in particular.

'I'll just go and make sure he's all right,' says Mum. She gives me a kiss. 'Don't worry about him, Mikey, and don't worry about me either, OK? We're both fine. We're a bit edgy right now, but we're not going to fall apart, and we're rock solid behind you. See you in a minute.'

And she disappears into the street. I watch her walk up to Dad and stand there with him in the middle of the road. They talk for a bit, neither looking this way, then she leads him over to the far pavement, and they go on talking, still not watching me. It's no good. However hard Mum tries to dress things up, they're both wrecked and I'm the cause of it. I go up to my room, walk over to the window, and stare out.

From downstairs comes the click of the front door as Mum and Dad come back in. I hear them go through to the kitchen, hear Mum start cooking again, then the clink of cutlery as Dad eats his meal, then they wander through to the front room, and their voices go quiet, which is good, because I don't want to hear what they're saying. I go on staring out of the window.

Denbury Close stays empty. If the gang are watching me, I can't see them, and I don't much care. They know where I live, which room I sleep in, even the wardrobe I hide in. They might as well be living here with me. I'm almost starting to think they are. I stay by the window, watching for Meggie to come back. I can't wait to see her, even though I'm going to disappoint her. At half-past four I see her running up Denbury Close, her eyes on my window. She gets her wave in before I manage mine. A few moments later she's through the front door and racing up the stairs. I meet her at my bedroom door and she reads my face with one glance.

'You're not coming,' she says.

I shake my head.

'Oh, Mikey, you said you'd try.'

'I know.'

'Straight after school,' she says. 'We agreed. Cup of tea and we'd head off to that place together.'

'I'm sorry, Meggie. I'm really . . .'

It's no good, I can't do it, and it's not just fear of that place. Everything's changed now, so much so that I'm not even sure I can bear to leave the house right now, or my bedroom. I glance towards the wardrobe. Or that. I feel Meggie's hand on my arm and look back at her. She's watching me tenderly, not saying anything, just showing me . . . I don't know . . . showing me something I don't deserve. She gives my arm a squeeze, and goes back downstairs. I walk over to the window again and stare out. Nobody visible in Denbury Close, just the cat making its leisurely way back towards our porch. I watch it for a moment, then turn away, pick up my mobile, and dive into the wardrobe.

CHAPTER 17

I don't come out for the rest of the day. By seven in the evening even Meggie's given up trying to coax me out. I keep the door closed and slump in the darkness, my phone still on. I've had texts pinging non-stop, all from the gang, all with the same message.

Ring mikey ring ring ring

But there's only one person I want to ring. Trouble is, I know Mr and Mrs Taylor-Hume will have taken Nip's mobile from him. He'll be in the doghouse after the incident at school and he won't be allowed near the landline either. If I ring that, I'll get Mr or Mrs T-H answering and they both hate me. Well, maybe they don't hate me, but they definitely disapprove of me as a friend for Nip. I think of their plush house, and my one and only visit there, for tea, when me and Nip were just getting friendly. I suppose I didn't help myself by freaking out with the light cutting in through those huge windows they've got, but it wasn't just that. They looked down on Dad too, when he dropped me off. They probably made their minds up as he parked our little banger alongside their big flash guzzlers.

I try Nip's mobile anyway. I've been putting it off all this time, half out of fear in case I do actually get through to him, because the truth is, I don't really know what I'm going to say to him if we get to speak. I know the bit I can say, the safe bit. I can say thank you for sticking up for me, mate, but that's the easy part. The other bit's so difficult I'm not sure I can even say it, or should say it. I just don't know. But I needn't have worried about his mobile. There's no answer and even voicemail's been turned off. I stare at the phone in the darkness. I almost wish the thing didn't work, or I could summon the power to switch it off, or I couldn't get a signal here in the wardrobe, or I had some excuse to avoid this. But it's no good. I find Nip's landline number, stare at it, press Call. Mr Taylor-Hume answers.

'Hello?'

Now that really is a voice. If the gang reckon I'm posh, they should listen to Mr Taylor-Hume, and Mrs Taylor-Hume's even worse. Luckily Nip talks like a normal human being, but I don't suppose I'll get a chance to hear him right now.

'Mr Taylor-Hume, it's Michael.'

'Michael,' he says, without expression.

'I was wondering if Nip's there.'

'He's not available at the moment.'

Mr Taylor-Hume's words might be stones falling on mud. I keep trying, even so.

'Is it possible he might be available some time later today?'

'No.'

'I see. OK, fair enough.'

There's a silence, which Mr Taylor-Hume makes no effort to break.

'Well,' I say, 'is there any chance you could maybe pass on a message?'

'I don't think so.'

'OK, all right.'

Another silence.

'Well, thank you anyway, Mr Taylor-Hume.'

The phone clicks off at the other end. Almost at once, another text comes in.

Mikey we aint gonna keep on being nice

Ping!

You gotta talk to us man

Ping!

We down by the corner shop come see us now

I switch off the phone, pull my knees into my chest, close my eyes. At nine o'clock Meggie comes up again. I hear her enter the room and call out.

'Mikey, I'm going to open the wardrobe door, all right?'

I don't answer. She calls out again.

'Is that all right, Mikey?'

'I don't want you to, Meggie.'

'Mikey, please.'

I hear Mum and Dad on the landing outside, but they don't come into my room.

'Mikey,' says Meggie, 'we just want you to come out.'

'I want to stay here, OK?'

This time Meggie's the one who doesn't answer. But I want her to.

'OK, Meggie?'

'OK, Mikey,' she says, and I hear her go.

A moment later they've all gone downstairs again. I switch my phone back on. As I expected, there's a stream of texts, all with the same message.

Getting really really impatient mikey

I switch off the phone again, push open the wardrobe door, listen. The television's on downstairs in the lounge. I crawl out, put my mobile on to charge, crawl back and lean against the side of the wardrobe. I'm glad none of the others left the light on in here. I need the darkness right now. All is quiet in my room, and out in Denbury Close, as usual. The sound of the television seems distant and alien. I think of the gang somewhere near. Maybe they were at the corner shop, maybe they weren't. I can't face the thought of them at all now. Wherever they are, I'm scared of them.

At half-past ten I hear Meggie coming up the stairs. I crawl back into the wardrobe and pull the door after me, but she doesn't come into my room, and a few moments later I hear her bedroom door close. An hour later Mum and Dad come up too. I hear the door to my room open, then a pause, presumably as they check to see if I'm in bed. I wait for one of them to try to coax me out, but Mum just calls, 'Goodnight, Mikey.'

'Goodnight,' I call back.

I hope they heard me. I didn't bother opening the wardrobe door. But they seem to accept it and disappear to their room. I wait for a while, then push open the wardrobe door, crawl out again, fetch my phone from the charger, and switch it on. Ping!

Look out the window mikey do it now

I make myself stand up and walk to the window. Below me, at the entrance to Denbury Close, are two figures. Hard to make out their faces but one of them looks like the guy who thrust the garden fork at me in Mr Gregory's shed. The other one's taller and he's holding a mobile phone. They seem to spot me straightaway because the taller one does a fancy little bow in my direction. Then he punches something into his phone. I wait for another text, but instead, my phone rings. I hesitate, my eyes on the two figures. They're motionless now, watching. I answer the phone.

'Yeah?' I say.

'Come down, Mikey.' It's the same mocking voice I heard before. 'Time for talking, baby.'

'We can talk on the phone.'

'No, we can't, man. Gotta talk face to face.'

'I'm not coming down.'

'Come down, Mikey. Don't make us get tough with you.'

'I'm not coming down. We can talk here on the phone.'

But my phone suddenly goes dead. I stare down at it, then at the street. The figure is punching a message. A moment later it appears.

Gonna be here thru the nite baby last chance

I pull the curtains across, switch off the phone, and throw myself on the bed. An hour later I'm still lying there, curled up. I make myself check round the side of the curtain. The two figures are still there, in exactly the same place, and they've now been joined by two more. I hurry past the bed and dive into the wardrobe again, and somehow, against all my expectations, I fall asleep. When I wake, it's morning, and I hear Meggie setting off for school. I stretch my arms, as far as the confines of the wardrobe allow me, and push open the door. Downstairs I hear the sound of Mum moving about the kitchen. I wander over to the window and check round the curtain. No figures, and Dad's car has gone. I hear Mum coming up the stairs. She stops outside my room, then knocks quietly.

'Come in, Mum,' I say.

She opens the door and smiles.

'Breakfast?' she says, as though all is well and nothing unusual has been happening.

'Yes, please,' I say, 'only, Mum—'

'You're not going in to school today,' she says. 'It's all right. I know you don't want to.'

'Thank you. I just—'

'Don't worry, Mikey. You'll be fine here today.'

But I'm not. I manage to keep out of the wardrobe but I can't get out of my room. Mum takes it all in her stride, brings my breakfast up on a tray, and then lunch, and a cup of tea in the early afternoon, and I sit here in my room, my mobile switched off, worrying because I know there are horrible messages waiting for me, and because hiding here isn't the answer, and because . . . something else is wrong, something I can't put my finger on. I just feel it. Maybe it's because I haven't see those figures again in Denbury Close. There's no reason why I should. They probably wouldn't stand there in broad daylight. But I'm worried about where they are and what they're doing. At three o'clock I hear Dad come home from work, several hours earlier than normal. He doesn't come up. I sit on the edge of the bed, switch on the phone, and wait for the ping—but there's nothing.

No message of any kind.

I stand up and walk to the window again, and stay there, looking out. The afternoon ticks on. I check my watch. Half an hour till Meggie gets back. I follow the minutes as they crawl by: 25, 20, 15, 10, 5, then at last it's time, and I see the bus chugging down Market Street towards the corner shop. I watch it slip past the bottom of the road and out of view to the place where it pulls over beyond the bakery, and I think of Meggie, and how she'll wave like she always does when she sees me watching from the window. Except suddenly I know that it's not going to happen. I can't explain why. All I know is that I'm staring out of the window at an empty space and I'm waiting not for Meggie but for something terrible; and here it is, right on cue. Ping! I hold up my mobile and read the text.

Cute little sister you got mikey want her back?

CHAPTER 18

I feel like I've been knifed. I stare at the words, then swish the curtains together, and slump back on the bed.

Ping!

Tell no one mikey or she gonna die

Ping!

And it gonna be messy

Ping!

Come on your own baby and dont tell nobody

I force myself to think. It could be bluff. They'd find it hard to get Meggie by herself. She'd have come out of school with one of her mates, Lucy, probably, or Gemma, or Sophie, or all them. There are twenty people she could have come out of school with, Ringo even, and they'd have walked out of the gate with her and down to the buses. She'd never have let those bastards trick her away from the group.

Ping!

You or little sis mikey your call

I've got thoughts pounding my head, and pictures of Meggie, and other things I can't bear to see. I jump up, yank open the door, run to the top of the landing, open my mouth to scream down, then stop. In the silence I hear Mum and Dad talking in the front room, just the tone, the worried tone, and that's all I need, because I'm leaning over the rail at the top of the stairs and I know I can't tell them, not just because I'll drown them with fear but because if the gang's not lying, then Meggie will be dead. There's only one solution to this. It's me and only me. They might just do a trade-off. The door of the front room opens and I hear Dad's voice.

'Meggie?'

I move back to keep out of sight. Dad walks into the hall and calls again.

'Meggie?'

Then Mum, still in the front room.

'She's not back yet.'

'I thought I heard the bus.'

'You did hear the bus.'

'Then where is she?'

'Don't ask me,' says Mum. 'Buying sweets from the corner shop probably.'

'She doesn't buy sweets,' I whisper.

'She doesn't buy sweets,' says Dad.

More footsteps below, as Mum comes out to join him in the hall.

'Then some of her friends have gone to buy sweets,' she says, 'and Meggie's gone with them.'

'She's not usually late,' says Dad.

I turn back into my room, shut the door, sit on the bed again. The darkness from the closed curtains falls around me. Ping!

Come and get her mikey.

Ping!

You no where 2 go

'Yeah,' I murmur, 'I know where to go.'

I straighten up, take a breath, gaze round the room, then slip on my shoes, run my hand over *Treasure Island*, walk to the desk, and scribble a note to Mum and Dad—then tear it into small pieces. It's no good. I can't tell them anything. I can't take the risk. They'll come looking for me the moment they read it, or call the police, or both, and the gang'll find out, and Meggie will die.

I think back to that place again and the day we went there, all because of my stupid bravado in insisting I could handle it, in spite of Meggie's doubts. I think of what happened there, and what's happened since, and what could happen next if I get this wrong. I'll never forgive myself if Meggie dies because of me, or if they do something terrible to her. I read the text again, press Reply.

Don't hurt her. I'm coming.

Send, switch off the phone, slip it in my pocket, creep back to the landing. Mum and Dad are still down in the hall. I can see them by the door. They've opened it and they're standing there, staring out into Denbury Close. They both look worried. I take a long breath, and another, then call down.

'Meggie won't be on the bus.'

They turn and peer up at me. I walk down the stairs, calm as I can.

'I'm meeting her in Castle Street,' I say.

'What?' says Mum.

'You didn't tell us,' says Dad.

Hard to tell if they believe me. They don't look like they do. I reach the hall and walk up to them.

'Sorry,' I say, 'should have told you. Another cock-up from me.'

Now they're really suspicious. I try to think of a way round this, but I'm an even worse liar than Mum.

'I got a text from Meggie,' I say. 'We agreed to meet up in Castle Street so we could go to that place again.'

'The secret place?' says Dad. 'The one you won't tell us about?'

'Yeah.'

They still look doubtful, but I keep trying.

'Meggie said it would be good for me to give it another go, since I freaked out a bit last time.'

'But you've been freaked out the last two days, Mikey,' says Mum. 'You've been stuck in your wardrobe and every-thing. You're not telling me Meggie's expecting you to meet up with her now and go off to a place you found so frightening before. She wouldn't force you to do some-thing like that when you've been so upset today.'

'And yesterday,' said Dad.

'She's not forcing me,' I say. 'I texted her back. Told her I was up for it.'

'You serious, Mikey?' says Dad.

'Yeah, I want to try again. I can't just bottle out when things get tough. So I told Meggie I'd meet her in Castle Street and we can go to that place again together, and she can leave me on my own for a bit and see if I can maybe do better than I did last time.'

How easy the lies are coming now I'm desperate to get away; and every second of standing here's making it worse, because I can see the doubts growing in their faces: doubts about me, about Meggie, about this whole pretence of a plan. They're never going to let me go. I'll have to wait for a chance later and slip out when they're not looking. Then Mum reaches out and pulls me to her.

'You're so brave, Mikey,' she says, 'you really are, and you never cease to amaze me.'

Dad's staying quiet but I can feel him watching my face.

'There's me worrying myself sick about you,' says Mum, 'and all the time you're trying your best to deal with things. I'm so proud of you, Mikey, and trust Meggie. That's so typical of her. I just wish one of you had told us about this, that's all, but never mind.'

She lets me go and steps back.

'Got everything you need?' she says.

I glance at Dad. He's still quiet, still watching. I pull my coat from the peg.

'Just this, Mum,' I say, slipping it on.

'Scarf?'

'No, I'm fine. It's not too cold.'

'Money?'

'Got it.'

Mum's looking worried again, even though she's talking upbeat. I can tell she doesn't think I'll manage this. She's probably right. Even the pretend plan feels beyond me. The light's already pushing in at me through the open front door. I scowl at the greedy brightness, but for once it doesn't hurt me so badly. Maybe it's because I've got a bigger predator to worry about. Not only that but darkness is coming on. Another hour and the day will be gone. I wonder what else will be gone too. I look at Dad again. He stays where is, still watching quietly.

'See you later, Dad.'

He says nothing. I turn to Mum, who smiles.

'Take care of yourself, Mikey,' she says. 'Got your mobile?'

'Yep.'

'All charged up?'

'Yep.'

'Ring us if you need to. We won't worry about you, OK?'

'Yeah, right.'

'Well, not very much.' She gives me a kiss. 'What time are you coming back?'

'No idea,' I say. 'I leave all the decisions to Meggie.'

Mum chuckles.

'So do we,' she says.

She glances at Dad. No chuckle from him, just a look.

'Mikey,' he says, 'where is this place you and Meggie are going?'

'Dad, it's—'

'A secret, I know,' he says, 'but I think you should tell us, just in case—'

'Dad, please.'

'Please what?'

I stare at him.

'Just please.'

I don't know what I'm asking him. I just know that whatever it is, I'm pleading for it, and he's watching me closer than ever, shaking his head now. That's when I know it's over and I'm not going. He'll never let me out of the house. He watches me for a while, silently, then turns briskly away.

'Come back safely, Mikey,' he says.

CHAPTER 19

I get to the corner shop OK, bent over like I normally am and shielding my eyes from the light. It's ripping into me the way it usually does, but so far I've kept at bay. Maybe that's because the thought of Meggie's taken over and it's dominating everything else. The light goes on stabbing me even so, the great sweeping space open all around me, specially now I'm out of Denbury Close and I've got Castle Street stretching away on both sides. I push it out of my mind and glance at the corner shop.

Mum was half-right about Meggie's friends. There's two in there right now, but they're not buying sweets. They're just talking to old Mr Blackwell, speaking loud to help him hear them, and it's nice stuff, friendly stuff, only I can't think of that now. I try to remember their names but it's no good. I've got to just try this and see how I go. I walk into the shop and up behind them. Mr Blackwell sees me first and smiles.

'Mikey,' he says, 'what can I do for you?'

The girls turn and see me. I flounder again for their names, give up, and dive in.

'Either of you seen Meggie?'

They shake their heads.

'You OK?' says one.

'Yeah, fine,' I say. 'Sorry, I've got to go.'

I spin round, hurry out of the shop, and I'm off down Castle Street, running now. Can't waste any more time. Every second could make a difference. Five minutes later I'm at the bus station, another five and I'm on Number 24, breathing hard, chest tight, the pictures of Meggie getting worse in my head. Into the city, past the stadium, darkness falling now, but the lights of the city bright around me. I've been putting off checking the mobile, but it won't do any longer. I pull it out, check it, and there's nothing.

I stare at it, trying to pretend I've got this whole thing wrong, that it's just a joke, a cruel joke, and the gang's only messing around, freaking me out for their own amusement, and they haven't got Meggie, she isn't in danger, and I'm not in danger either. It's just a sick piece of fun. They know I can't hurt them, they know I won't say anything or do anything, and that I just want to stay in my wardrobe and not cause them any trouble, and when I get back home, I'll find Meggie there wondering where I've been.

Ping!

The usual number.

I luv u big guy m x

I stare at the message.

'Oh, Jesus.'

'You OK, fella?' says a voice.

I turn and see an old man's watching me: tatty coat, scarf, eccentric kind of hat. He smiles.

'You muttered something, fella. Just wondered if you're OK.'

I turn away. Can't find the words to speak to him, and anyway, here's my stop. I get off the bus, keep my back to it, wait till I hear it drive off. Don't want to see that old guy's face. I know he's kind, I know he's probably watching me, ready to smile again, but I don't want to see him. I just want him gone. But the sound of the bus soon goes. It's been drowned by the din from Switchback City Funfair. I look down at the text again.

I luv u big guy m x

I'm trying to find a reason why this didn't come from Meggie, and I can see one already. She's finicky about punctuating and capitalizing and writing proper English, even in texts. She's funny like that. Gets it from Dad. She'd never write *luv u*. She'd write it in normal English. Somebody else must have written the text. But even as I'm thinking this, I know it's crap. If they've got her, then God knows what state she's in, and what kind of thing she'd write.

I hurry towards the gate into the funfair, keeping the phone on, even though I'm terrified of what'll come through next. I reach the gate and stop, people pushing past me on their way in and out. Same old guy in the booth as when I came with Meggie before. If he recognizes me, he doesn't show it, just takes the money and turns to the next person as I slip through. I stop just inside the entrance, and look around.

It could have worked, this plan, if we'd kept to Meggie's idea: take Mikey somewhere he's never been, somewhere safe but out of his comfort zone, stay with

111

him and help him get used to it, then, when he says he's ready, leave him on his own in an agreed spot for an agreed amount of time, and then meet up again and take him home. Yeah, it could have worked. If I hadn't insisted we come to this bloody place, with its noise and crowds and flashing lights. If I hadn't acted the hero that I'm never going to be.

And if it hadn't been for the gang.

I wonder where they are now. Hard to believe they'll be keeping Meggie at the place I first saw them. It's surely too public. But what else can I do? I think of their text. *You no where 2 go.* They've got to mean here. They tried getting to me at school, and then at home, and neither worked, so now they're making me come to them here, where the trouble all started. I look about me, fighting the open space, the din, the glare, and again I try to tell myself this is a joke, and Meggie's safe, and there's no one here waiting for me, no one watching, as I start to walk through the funfair. But there is.

I can feel the gang, even if I can't see them. I sense the space again too, the opening-closing space, gaping and smothering with its cold emptiness. Even the brittle lights of the funfair can't breach it. The noise and the crowds only make it worse. I'm watching faces now, searching for the ones I've seen before and somehow must see again, and Meggie's face, the thing I want more than anything. But she won't be here among the rides and slides and food stalls. I'm not even confident she'll be where they say she is, but I walk on anyway, past the hot dogs and toffee apples and candyfloss stands, the ferris wheel and bumper cars and bouncy castles, and the

112

Twister and the Mirror Maze, and on to the great Terror Ride, the last and greatest piece of craziness here: the place where Meggie left me and I was supposed to wait.

If only I had done.

I stare up at it for a moment, the great rollercoaster, gaudy with lights, and at the small moving dot rising and plunging at its far end—but I want no more of this. It was the sight of that racing box of screams that drove me away last time, and it might as well do so again. I hurry off the way I went before, round the back of the Terror Ride to the deserted edge of the park where there's nothing but litter and broken bottles, and the tall perimeter fence rising before me, and darkness, big, heavy darkness. It felt like an escape last time, from the noise, the lights, the people, the hungry space, the box of screams hurtling round. It's drawing close again. I can't miss the sound of it, rattling and roaring high above me, even though I've turned so I can't see it.

The screams of the thrill-seekers come stinging down, digging so sharply into me that I cry out in spite of myself, but then suddenly they're gone, and the moving box has raced by, and it's just me and the darkness again, and the tall perimeter fence. I walk slowly towards it, the grass strewn with beer cans and sweet wrappers. Somewhere far away the box of screams is slowing down, and then the sound ceases altogether, and somehow in the absence of it the cacophony of the funfair feels almost like silence. I walk up to the fence. It feels horribly familiar, but maybe that's just the words paint-sprayed on the timbers, some accompanied by drawings, just as hard to forget. I follow them down towards the farthest point where the fence turns back the other way, and then I stop.

No one's here. I didn't expect the gang. If they're waiting anywhere, it'll be where they were when I first saw them, not the place from where I was watching. But I can't put this off any longer. I walk up to the giant cartoon at the farthest end of the fence. I'm not really seeing the bloated body with the sagging breasts, the lifted skirt, the splayed legs. I'm not even seeing the words that tell us what she comes here for. I'm seeing in my mind the hidden cul-de-sac beyond with its long blank wall and the closed garages at the far end where the lane curls round and goes no further; and here's the gap in the fence, the size of my face, between the lady's legs.

I lean close and peer through it.

CHAPTER 20

There's nobody there, nobody to be seen anyway. I suppose they could be hiding either side of the gap, somewhere out of view, but I don't think so. To be honest, I never expected to see anyone here, just the shadows of what I saw before. I picture them now, over by the garages: six of them, four guys, two girls, all about seventeen. I could tell that even though it was as dark then as it is now, but the big deal wasn't their age. It was something much more serious, and now the big deal is even bigger: it's Meggie. For me she's all that matters. I don't care about anything else. So where the hell are they? I've come running like they told me to and they're not here. My mobile rings. I stare down at the flashing word.

HOME.

How far away that seems. I can't speak to Mum and Dad. I won't handle it. I wait till voicemail cuts in, give them enough time to say their bit, then play back the message. It's Mum.

'Hi, darlings. Just checking you're both OK.'

Both, she said both. Shit, so Meggie's not back.

'Hope you're having a good time,' says Mum. 'No need to rush back, long as everything's OK, but can you just text us to let us know you're all right? Thanks. Love you both.'

And she rings off. Behind me the Terror Ride starts again and I hear the box of screams zigzagging its way back round the switchback towards me. I stare through the gap again, searching the little cul-de-sac. Still no one there. Yet again I think back to what I should have done. If I'd moved more quickly, I could have got away without being seen. But I stood at the gap too long. I saw what I saw, and then I lingered, unable to break away, and in that time they saw my face; well, one particular person did.

And that was the game changer.

For me, for the gang, and now for Meggie. I saw what I saw, and then I got seen, and recognized. I don't know what happened next, don't have it clear in my mind. I remember being freaked out, and I must have turned away somehow because the next thing I can picture for certain is Meggie finding me wandering round the base of the Terror Ride with the bloody great screamy thing rattling over my head, and I'm out of my brain and mumbling, and she's saying something about me not being in the place we agreed to meet, and then she's pulling me away out of the funfair, and somehow or other we end up home—and now they've got Meggie, the most precious part of my life, and it's all because of me, and I just want them to take me instead and let Meggie live.

Ping!

I jump at the sound. It almost feels louder than the box of screams careering over me, and certainly more terrifying. I stare at the phone. Can't bring myself to open the text straightaway. Could be Mum and Dad, could be the gang. I want it to be the gang. It is.

Walk out the funfair mikey

I start walking, out of the shadowy glade behind the Terror Ride and through the scaffolding into the noisy crowd. I'm staring round now, searching faces again. Walk out, they said, so they know I'm here and that means they're here too, or some of them are. I go on searching faces. Nobody familiar but everyone looks like an enemy now.

Ping!

I stop, jostled on all sides. What more do these bastards want? I'm going, aren't I? I'm walking out like they said. Can't get there any quicker with all these people blocking the way. I open the text.

Everything ok? Mum and Dad xxx

They're worrying now. I knew they would be. That upbeat message from Mum was always hiding something. I try to think. Mustn't say too much or I'll give everything away, and I can't let them stop me now. I've got to go through with this. It's the only chance for Meggie. One word will do. I key it in.

Fine.

Look over it, take a breath, key in some more.

Fine. Don't worry.

Look over it again. I feel such a bastard.

Fine. Don't worry. We love you. M & M xxx

Send.

And I still feel a bastard. Because this might be the last thing they ever get from either of us, and it's a lie, and I wrote it. The mobile pings again.

Get a move on mikey

I'm shoving people aside now, getting angry glances, but I don't care. I just want this whole thing to be over. I'm past the Terror Ride, running when I can, though the spaces soon close up as more people crowd in, and now I'm past the Twister and the Mirror Maze, and there's kids with mums and dads and grannies and grandpas, all happy laughing faces, people I'm never going to see again, people who don't know the boy hurrying past them is almost certainly racing to his death.

If they see me at all, which they probably don't, and it doesn't matter now anyway, because I'm in front of the entrance at last, and the old guy's still there in the booth by the turnstile, and he even looks at me again, and, like before, shows no recognition. I'm going to die unremembered, unnoticed, and maybe Meggie is too, if she's not already dead. I stop by the turnstile and stare out beyond the entrance. People milling about there too, some waiting to come in, some just out, but nobody who looks like the member of a gang.

I push through out of the funfair, and look around me. Lots of figures still hanging about, talking, laughing, others moving off, some towards the bus stop. I stare down at it. No bus there at the moment but I can hear one rumbling down from further up the road. A moment later it appears. Number 14. It'll take me most of the way home if I jump on it. The bus pulls in to the stop and, as it does so, I feel something close over my eyes: the cold, moist hands of someone standing behind me. Then I hear a guy's voice. It's familiar from down by the brook.

'Not your bus, Mikey. You want the next one. It's just coming in. Number 37. Go all the way to the end. And Mikey . . . ' A pause. 'Tell no one. Or she dies.'

The hands vanish as quickly as they came, but before I can look round, they've shoved me hard in the back and I'm stumbling forward. I keep my balance somehow and stare round, but there's no one to be seen, no one to recognize anyway, just the endlessly changing parade of faces entering and leaving the funfair. I turn back to the bus stop.

And see a Number 37 pulling in.

CHAPTER 21

I sit on the bus, staring out. I know where Number 37 ends up and I don't want to think about it. I check round. Plenty of other passengers but no one from the gang. I think of how those bastards have found their way into my life, how they've taken it over, how they're probably going to bring it to an end, and all because I saw what I saw and didn't have the sense to run away in time. But I don't matter. I absolutely don't matter. Meggie's all that matters.

I picture her face as the bus rumbles on. We'll be half an hour getting there and I might as well spend the time visualizing the person I love most. I try not to see her as she might be now. I can't bear to think of that. I try to picture her with that smile she's got, when she's chivvying me along, or bigging me up, or fixing something I can't deal with, or pulling my leg. I picture her so keenly it pushes everything else away. Even as I stare out of the window, I see Meggie's face in the reflection of my own from the glass.

'I'm sorry, Meggie,' I murmur.

I listen for her voice in my head, that strong voice that kept raging inside me, driving me on, but my head's silent now. I guess I just imagined it after all. I wanted it, willed it, pretended it, but it was all an illusion and I don't have any courage after all, certainly not Meggie's. It's hers alone, hers to keep, and there's one thing I know for certain: if they've hurt her and killed her, she'll have faced it a thousand times better than I could have done.

'I'm sorry,' I murmur again.

The bus pulls into Remembrance Square and starts to circle the Memorial Stone. It's got tourists wandering around it, most of them with cameras and stuff. Chinese, Japanese, can't tell, and I don't know why I'm even thinking about them. We're soon past and Remembrance Square's behind us and we're roaring down Pennsylvania Avenue towards Broad Park. I can see St Florian's church on the left, its spire brightly lit, but it looks ghostly and cold. The bus pulls over at the entrance to Broad Park. No one gets off; couple of people get on. I check the faces again, but still nobody from the gang. I almost wish there was, and I wish the mobile would send me another message. Ping! I look down at the phone.

HOME.

Mikey, please text or ring to let us know you're both ok.

The bus starts to move off again, past the entrance to Broad Park and on towards the river. I try to think. I could phone Mum and Dad, just phone them, do the thing. Maybe it's what I should have done from the start: told them what I saw in the cul-de-sac outside the fun-fair, what happened afterwards, the emails, the texts, all that stuff, and what's happened since, including today. I could tell them everything, throw it all on to them. Except Meggie'll die. She'll just die. Because there's still a chance she could be alive, and I could maybe save her, if I trade myself in for her.

I've got to believe in that, so I've got to do what they say: keep quiet and turn up. That's the point, and it's been the point all along: I've got to do what they say. They hold all the cards. I've got to chance it and hope they'll swap Meggie for me. Not much else I can do now. I've messed things up from the start. I didn't run when I had the chance to get away unrecognized and I didn't say anything to anyone when they started bombarding me with emails, because I thought if I just hide away in my wardrobe, they'll go away and take the problem and the threats with them.

So I've been a coward. That's basically it. A useless effing coward. And now they've got Meggie, and me, and it's all my fault. So I can't ring Mum and Dad now, because it's too late. They'll phone the police straight away and it'll be over for Meggie. It probably already is. But I've got to try this, got to do what I can. I tap another text to Mum and Dad.

All ok. M and M x

Send.

I stare out of the window again. We're passing the museum and rumbling on towards the east side of the city.

Ping!

All the way to the end mikey

I'm going, aren't I, you bastards? No need to tell me twice.

The bus rolls on through darker streets, pulling in to stops and out again, and now it's turning right, towards the docks. I've never been to the last stop. It's not a place I'd ever want to go. Another ten minutes and I'm getting glimpses of the water as the warehouses on the south side of the river fall away. The other buildings are getting fewer too, and so are the passengers. Mostly empty seats now, apart from some women on the back row, and an old guy on my right. We pull over by the supermarket and they all get off.

Nobody gets on. The driver glances round, looks me over like he's wondering if I really want to go all the way to the end, then he closes the doors, and we drive on. The last stop soon appears. I see it well in advance, the old bus shelter where this heap of metal will turn round and head back into the city without me, and where the lane by the pub cuts down to the dockland buildings and the river beyond. I've already worked out that's the way I'll be going.

I stare out of the window at the shelter drawing near, and the pub, and the lane. There's no sign of a welcoming party, no sign of anyone at all, even waiting for the bus back to the city. The lights of the pub are off too. Looks boarded up. The bus pulls in, stops, the driver glances round at me again, and there's that same question in his face: what the hell are you doing getting off here? I stand up and walk to the door of the bus. Least I haven't got daylight to fight now as well as everything else, but the space outside still yawns like a great maw. I get ready to plunge into it, when the driver calls out.

'You OK, kid?'

I turn and look at him. He gives me what I think is a smile: not much of a one but I'm grateful for it. I give him a nod, then stare out of the door again. The maw widens, like it wants to devour me. I almost wish it would. There's nobody out there waiting. All I can see in the giant mouth is the rusty outline of the bus shelter, the drabness of the pub, the lane reaching into the darkness in the direction of the docks. I step off the bus, hear the door close behind me, the engine rev up again. I glance round and watch. The driver's turning, his eyes on the wheel, the road, the job in hand, and now he's heading back towards the city. He flashes a final look at me but doesn't slow down.

I turn back to the lane and see two shadows at the top.

CHAPTER 22

Guys, hooded, but I recognize both of them from the build. They were sitting on the motorbike last time I saw them. Maybe it's something in the shoulders. Doesn't matter. I know who they are. They don't call out or beckon. They just wait and watch. I stay where I am for the moment, try to let the darkness settle me, but it stays tight against my eyes. I guess I should be glad it's not cutting into me like the sunlight does. I couldn't handle that as well right now. I walk towards the two figures.

They haven't moved. They're just standing there, close to the right-hand wall of the lane. Don't know why I didn't spot them before, but maybe they were hanging about further down and only came up when they heard the bus pull in. They were obviously watching out for it. I keep walking, thinking of Meggie, and how much braver she'd be than I am right now, because I can't stop myself trembling, no matter how hard I try, and they'll have noticed that, even in the darkness.

Probably makes them feel good, seeing me like this. I keep going somehow and stop in front of them. They look me over, hoods still up, and I try to make out their faces. But all I can see is the eyes of the guy on my right. They're familiar, though. I remember seeing them when he raised the visor of his helmet as he stared down at me from the back of the motorbike: hard, bullety eyes. He speaks suddenly.

'You gave us a V-sign, Mikey.'

I don't answer.

'Not very friendly,' he says.

'Where's Meggie?'

Bulleteyes just looks at me. Then his mate thrusts out a hand.

'Mobile,' he says to me.

I stare back at him. He snaps his fingers.

'Mobile, give me your mobile!'

I squeeze it tight. Somehow it feels like all I've got left. I don't care about my wallet or my keys, but the mobile . . .

'Give it!' he yells.

I hold it out. He snatches it from me, stuffs it in his pocket, and sticks out his hand again.

'The rest.'

'What?'

'Everything else you got, give it!'

There's no point arguing. I hand him my wallet and keys, and he stuffs those away too. Bulleteyes nods me down the lane.

'Move.'

I stay put.

'Move!' he says.

'I've come like you told me to.'

'So what do you want?' he says. 'Bunch of flowers?'

'Listen—'

'To what, posh boy?'

'You said you had questions and I know what they're about. You want to know what I saw and if I've said anything to anyone.'

Neither of them answers me and I hurry on.

'I saw you and your gang in that cul-de-sac by the funfair, OK? But I didn't see what was going on. It was too dark. So whatever you were doing, I didn't see it, and I haven't said anything to anybody, not even my family, not even my sister, so you're safe. You and your gang are safe.'

I don't know if they're buying any of this. Maybe they've guessed I'm lying or maybe it doesn't matter and they're going to kill me anyway, to make sure, or just for fun. I know what they can do, because I've watched them do it. But I keep trying.

'I don't want any trouble, OK? And my sister's got nothing to do with any of this. We just want to go home and forget the whole thing and keep our mouths shut. So you can stop worrying, because we're not going to say anything to the police.'

Bulleteyes flicks his hood down, and I recognize the face straight away from the cul-de-sac that night: lean, unshaven, close-cropped hair. I remember what he did too, and how much he enjoyed it.

'We ain't worried about you talking to the police, posh boy,' he says, ''cos you ain't gonna get a chance.' He pauses. 'Neither of you.'

'Where's Meggie?'

'You'll find out soon enough.'

'Haven't got her, have you?'

The moment the words are out I wish I hadn't said them. The guy with my phone flicks his own hood down, and there's another familiar face from the cul-de-sac: smooth skin, greasy hair. It was these two did most of the damage that night, together with the guy who shoved the garden fork at me in Mr Gregory's shed. The girl who was with him, the one with the lip piercings, was in the thick of it too in the cul-de-sac. The fourth guy there that night must be the one I spoke to on the phone, the smarmy one with the mocking laugh. As for the sixth member of the gang, the other girl, I'm not expecting to see her tonight.

She'll keep well away from this. I'm sure of it.

Greasy looks at Bulleteyes, then at me, then keys in a number on my phone and puts it to his ear. A pause, and he speaks.

'It's me.' Another pause while he listens to someone, then, 'Yeah, he is.' He looks me over and says, 'Stick the girl on.'

Then he holds out the phone. I take it and put it to my ear. I'm dreading what I'm going to hear, specially after taunting these two a moment ago about them not having Meggie, but right now there's silence at the other end of the line: no voices, no background noise, no clue of anything. I start to wonder—yet again—if this could still be some hideous joke, some sick piece of fun these people are having with me, and when they've made sure I'm as scared as I possibly can be and they're bored with the whole thing, they'll let me go with a clipped ear, and I'll find out Meggie was at home after all. Then I hear her voice.

'Mikey?'

I scream back into the phone.

'Meggie!'

But it's snatched away from me.

'Give it back!' I yell.

Greasy's already tucking the thing in his pocket. I throw myself at him, dig my hand in after it, but he pushes me away easily, then Bulleteyes grabs me from behind. I turn my head and bawl at him.

'Let me speak to her!'

'Sure you can speak to her,' he says, 'no problem at all.'

He nods again down the lane.

'Like I said before, posh boy: move.'

I start walking down the lane, the two of them just behind. They don't talk and I'm glad of that. I've got to steel myself for whatever's coming. The lane's deserted, walls on either side with just the shadows of warehouses beyond, and the occasional gleam of water further down. I can hear the hum of the city farther off, but it sounds like the song of another planet, nothing to do with this place, then the hum falls away and we walk on through silence; and in that silence, I hear Meggie's voice again, in my head, but not as it should be, not as it always has been. I hear it as I just heard it in the phone a few moments ago: a frozen, terrified voice. I never want to hear my name spoken that way again.

The lane's widening now, and bending to the right, and then left again, still walls on either side, and now it's joining a bigger road, and here are the docks opening before us. The main entrance is closed, but I don't suppose we were ever going in that way, if we're going in at all, and sure enough they're pushing me off the road altogether now, through a broken-down section of the wall, and heading over a field, if you can call this scrawny patch of ground a field.

Over a rickety fence and into another field, tracking the river as we go. I can see it easily now, running to our left, silky and bright, in spite of the darkness, and we're heading east, leaving behind us the dockland buildings and derricks and quaysides and containers. I feel a tap on my shoulder and look round. Greasy points towards the bottom of the field. I turn back and see a small stile in the far corner, leading not to another field, but to a path along the river itself. I walk down to it, climb over, and wait. Greasy and Bulleteyes climb over too, then, without ceremony, they stop me.

'This is for the V-sign, Mikey,' says Bulleteyes.

And they fall on me.

CHAPTER 23

When I come to, everything's black. I don't remember much. I just know I'm aching all over my body and my head's pounding. I don't know where I am. But I'm on the ground and I'm curled up, and I've got some kind of hood over my head, and it's tied there. My hands are tied too, behind my back. I give a moan, move my mouth. No gag. I suppose that's something, but not much. Probably only means they're confident we're too far away for anyone to hear us. I listen.

Nothing, not even distant traffic, or the ripple of the river, if that's still near us. I could be anywhere. I vaguely remember being carried, or rather bundled along, probably on someone's back, but I might have got that wrong, because I think I blacked out more than once. Not that it matters. I'm going to die anyway. They don't want to talk. They want to take no chances and finish me. One thing still matters, though, and it matters very much.

'Meggie?' I murmur.

There's no answer. I listen again, try to gauge where I am. Can't feel the breeze on my body, and there was a breath of wind earlier. I felt it when I was crossing the field, specially as we got close to the water. I call a little louder.

'Meggie?'

Still nothing, and then I black out again. Next time I come round I hear voices. Can't make them out too well, I'm still a bit dazed, but there's definitely three guys and one girl, and they sound tense, all pitching in together.

'She's useless. She's pathetic.'

'Waste of space.'

'She ain't one of us.'

'We give her one last chance, OK?'

'But she shouldn't be in the gang, man.'

'We give her one last chance.'

'She could bring us down.'

'Specially now we know the guy died.'

They mutter on for a bit and I lose the words. Then I catch them again.

'So, listen, we all agreed?'

'Not happy about this.'

'We give her one last chance.'

'And if she messes up?'

'We know what to do.'

More muttering, but I hear some sort of agreement. I try to make out where they are. They sound like they're on the other side of a wall. Maybe I'm inside some building and they're on the outside. They go on talking, same kind of stuff, and I'm getting the picture. I know the girl they're talking about. I wasn't expecting to see her here, but maybe I will now, if she's got to prove herself to them, and I know about the guy who died too.

132

But I always knew about him. I just wiped the whole thing out of my mind, like the weak little coward I am. I pretended it wasn't there, but I knew. I knew it when I went downstairs to the kitchen that time and Mum switched off the radio news and said, 'Doom and gloom'. I'd heard the end of the report before I entered the kitchen so I knew about the guy who died in the cul-de-sac by Switchback City Funfair, and even then I tried to pretend it wasn't the man I saw. I can't believe what a shit I am, how spineless, how worthless.

I should have done something. I don't know what, but something. I picture the old man again, what I could make out of him anyway in the darkness. He wasn't dead then, not when I stuck my face to the gap in the fence and peered through into the cul-de-sac. He was sprawled on the ground in front of the garages but he was still moving, just, as the gang took his money and then kicked out. I'm starting to recognize the voices now, and put faces to them. They're not all out there, I don't think, but I've got names for the whole gang now.

Bulleteyes and Greasy, the two who knocked me out for the V-sign; Forkman, who wanted to stab my eye out in Mr Gregory's shed; and Lippygirl, the one with the lip piercings who was with him. Smarmy, the guy with the mocking laugh I spoke to on the phone, doesn't seem to be here right now, and there's one more gang member missing too: the one they've been talking about, the one who's got to prove herself. The girl I saw and recognized, and who saw and recognized me, that night at Switchback City Funfair. Lippygirl mentions her name with scorn in her voice.

'No point waiting for Nell,' she says. 'She ain't coming.'

'We wait for Nell,' says Bulleteyes. 'We agreed. We give her one last chance.'

I think of Nip's wayward sister and the few times I've seen her. She wasn't at Nip's house when I went there to tea on that one awkward occasion, and she's hardly ever been in school. When she is, she's usually in trouble with teachers or other pupils, or both, though never with Nip, and never with me. She knows me as Nip's friend and I know her as Nip's sister, but that's it. We've never spoken and never wanted to, and I certainly don't want to now. I just want to see Meggie and tell her I love her, while I've still got a chance.

The darkness inside the hood seems to deepen. Part of me hopes they'll never take it off. It's the only thing left that comforts me, and for a moment I almost feel like I'm curled up in the wardrobe, but that's fading already, because I know time's short. I try to work out where Meggie is. I'm terrified that she's already dead, but if she's still alive, she must be with Nell or Smarmy. The thought of her with either horrifies me. The talk goes on outside, then I hear a new guy's voice, further off.

'Got him?'

Nobody answers. I listen, trying to work out this new arrival. It's got to be Smarmy, unless there's another gang member I didn't see that night. Then I hear it, the laugh, and it kindles a sick new memory in my head, because I've heard it not just in the earpiece of my phone but that night in the cul-de-sac: the long, unending snigger, as the old man started to die; and now Smarmy's drawing close, talking and chuckling as he comes, and the other voices are coming closer too, some of them laughing with him, and suddenly it's all happening too quickly and I haven't got time to prepare myself. I feel legs pressed against me, hands clipping the top of my head, and I know I've got to talk fast.

'You've got to let us go,' I say, 'me and my sister.'

I hear their breathing close around me. I rush on.

'Meggie doesn't know anything about this and I didn't see anything in the cul-de-sac, OK? I told you before. So we can't hurt you. You've got to let us go.'

'Ain't gonna happen, posh boy,' says Forkman.

'You said you wanted to talk.'

'We don't want to talk,' says Bulleteyes.

'You said you did. In all your messages.'

'We was lying,' says Smarmy. 'We just wanted to check you ain't told no one what you saw and who you saw doing it.'

'I haven't told anyone, and I won't, and neither will Meggie.'

'We know that, Mikey,' says Bulleteyes. 'That's why you're here. So we can make sure you won't.'

'Listen—'

'No, man,' says Bulleteyes. 'We ain't come here to listen. It's simple, OK?'

He pauses, then speaks again.

'You and your sister gotta die.'

That's when I hear the final voice. It comes from somewhere further off, I'm guessing the door to whatever this place is: a hard, aggressive voice, worse even than Lippygirl's. I think of the times I've heard it at school, when Nell was slagging off another pupil, or a teacher, or sticking up for Nip; because there was at least one good thing you could say about Nell: she loves her little brother. But there's no love in her voice right now: just dark, violent anger.

'You got him?' she snarls, ''cos I ain't come all this way just for a walk.'

Her voice sounds strange, as though she's coarsened not just her original accent but the words too. Even when I've heard her screaming at a teacher or another pupil, she's never used words like 'ain't'. Bulleteyes answers her.

'Yeah, we got him, Nell. You up for this?'

'Course I am,' says Nell.

'We don't want you bottling out again.'

'I ain't bottling out,' says Nell. 'What are you talking about? He's seen too much. So we finish it.'

'We got his sister too.'

'You what?'

'We got his sister too.'

There's a silence from Nell. Smarmy pipes up.

'Only way we could get the boy here, Nell. So you know what that means, right?'

Another silence, but only a short one, before Nell comes raging back.

'Course I do,' she says. 'Let's get on with it.'

'I'll go get her,' says Smarmy.

And I hear him go. The others don't talk but I feel them stay close around me. I try not to think of them and focus on the sound I'm yearning to hear, and then it comes: footsteps from the direction that Smarmy went, and I can tell it's not him. He's there too, but he's not alone. The footsteps move slowly towards me and stop, then a hand touches the top of my hood, another my shoulder.

And I know it's Meggie.

CHAPTER 24

I feel the hood slowly removed, and there she is, in front of me. I straighten up, ignoring the shadowy forms of the gang members standing round us, and stare into Meggie's face. She has no hood, no hands tied, and she's still in her school uniform, and for a moment, in the darkness, it's almost as though I'm seeing her at home, in my room, looking at me with that familiar earnest gaze. But the fantasy soon fades as I see the bruises on her face, the blood round her mouth, the mess of her hair, the rumpling of her school uniform. Her eyes are fixed on mine, but they have an inward look, as though she's watching me from a long way back. She doesn't speak; she just looks at me.

'Meggie, I'm sorry,' I whisper.

She moves, not sharply, almost with hesitation, as though she's no longer sure what she can do and what she can't, then her arms slip round my back and pull me close. I want to hug her back, but I can't with my hands tied, but now she's reaching down and pulling at the knots. I wait for one of the gang members to stop her but no one does. I sense their impatience, though, and I know this won't last. Meggie unties the knots at last and the rope falls free. I reach quickly round her and hold her tight.

'Ah, ain't that sweet,' says Smarmy, and I hear the sick laugh.

The others join in but Nell steps briskly forward.

'Let's move this on,' she rasps.

The gang crowd round and I feel my arms ripped away from Meggie and hers from me, then a hand seizes me by the hair and yanks me to my feet. Someone's already done the same to Meggie and she's being bundled through the darkness towards a pale open doorway. Smarmy's got me by the hair and he's hurrying me forward after her, but then suddenly he stops and jerks me round to face the black poky hole I've been in.

'Sorry we couldn't find you a wardrobe, Mikey,' he sniggers, 'but we done our best.'

I stare round at the place. I know what it is now: a Second World War pillbox. Probably they were keeping Meggie in one of the others. I remember hearing there are lots round this part of the river. But there's no time to think. Smarmy's already whirled me round to the doorway again and I can see the rest of the gang gathered outside. Forkman's got Meggie's hair locked in a tight grip.

'Let her go!' I yell at him.

He turns, sees me being bundled out of the pillbox, and gives me the finger. Smarmy pushes me through the open doorway, then kicks me forward, but I'm still glaring at Forkman.

'Let her go, you bastard!'

'Whatever you say,' says Forkman.

He lets Meggie go, strides forward, and slams his fist into the side of my face. I feel the darkness crash inside my head and a moment later I thud to the ground. When I come to, I see Meggie bending over me. She's wiping blood from my face with one hand and cradling my head with the other. I see the sky moving blackly above her.

'Mikey,' she whispers, but she can say no more.

I whisper back.

'I'll take care of you, Meggie.'

I feel strange saying that, not just because I can't honour such a promise, but because it's always been the other way round; Meggie's always taken care of me. But if it feels strange to Meggie too, she gets no chance to show it. Nell's face thrusts itself into my line of vision, and Greasy's, and Forkman's, and then Smarmy's, grinning like he's watching a freak show. He gives my face a little slap, then does the same to Meggie.

'You two are just so cute, you know?'

Nell pushes him aside.

'We're wasting time,' she says. 'Get 'em apart.'

Forkman pulls Meggie back from me, his eyes daring me to say something again. Meggie's eyes have turned away, even from me. Bulleteyes comes over and grabs me by the collar.

'Time to move, posh boy,' he says, and he hauls me back to my feet.

Lippygirl joins him.

'Best to tie 'em up again and put the hoods back on,' she says, 'and gag 'em too.'

140

Bulleteyes shakes his head.

'Might attract attention,' he says. 'Not that there's likely to be anyone where we're going.'

Lippygirl glances at me, then back at Bulleteyes.

'So what if we do see someone and this boy calls out?' she says. 'Or the girl does?'

'They won't say a word,' says Nell.

She flicks open a knife, steers the blade towards my face, then stops it, an inch away. I stare down it and along Nell's arm, and past her to the others. Forkman's still got Meggie by the hair, but he's turned her round so she's watching me. Nell glowers at me along the blade.

'You call out, Mikeyboy, and she gets it.'

She turns to face Meggie.

'And you call out, he gets it.'

She snaps the knife shut and steps back.

'Everybody clear?'

I don't answer. Neither does Meggie. But I don't think we need to.

'Good,' says Nell. 'Now let's get going.'

Greasy and Bulleteyes have already set off down a slope I don't recognize. They must have carried me up it after they knocked me out. Forkman's just behind them with Meggie. He's let go of her but he's standing close and giving her the occasional push in the back. He doesn't need to, the bastard—she's doing as she's told—but I don't dare yell at him again. Could be worse for Meggie if I do that. Smarmy shoves me in the back too and I stumble after them. A moment later I feel two shadows either side of me, Smarmy on the left, Lippygirl on the right.

Lippygirl's got a knife out too now, and she's making sure I see it. I glance at Smarmy. First time I've had a proper look at him. He's smooth, that's for sure, but he's dangerous too, no missing that. He didn't do quite as much of the heavy stuff as the others in the cul-de-sac, but he won't hesitate to kill me if he has to, only it won't be with a knife. It'll be with a gun, because he's got one on him and, like Lippygirl, he's made sure I've seen what he's carrying. God knows what the rest of the gang have got.

I glance round at Nell. She's walking behind me, quiet for the moment, staring down at the ground. I can't imagine what she must have done to get into a gang like this. They must know she comes from a background way more posh than anything me and Meggie know about. But she looks like one of them, that's for sure. I check her over, with her short-cropped, bleach-blonde hair, her tattoos, her rough nails, some varnished, some not, and wonder what Nip would think if he could see his sister right now and know what she's planning to do tonight. Nell seems to sense me watching and looks up.

'What are you staring at?' she growls.

Before I can answer she rushes forward and punches out at me. I duck and her fist slides past my cheek, but her other arm whirls round and hooks me by the throat.

'Don't stare at me, you shit!' she snaps.

'Nell,' says Forkman, 'not now.'

She goes on glaring into my eyes.

'Nell,' calls Bulleteyes, 'save it for later!'

Nell thrusts me away, then spits into my face.

'Keep your eyes off me, all right?'

I turn away, wiping my face, and see that the others have all stopped, their eyes moving from me to Nell. I see Meggie watching too, her face as haunted as before. From behind me comes the sound of Nell breathing hard. I keep my back to her. Bulleteyes and Greasy start walking again, Forkman shoves Meggie forward, and we move on down the slope. Lippygirl and Smarmy stay either side of me, as close as before, but Nell's clearly had enough of being at the back. With a baleful stare in my direction, she thrusts past and on to Forkman and Meggie, and then past them to Bulleteyes and Greasy. The two guys turn as she approaches but she simply strides past them and takes the lead. I look ahead to where she's taking us and see a small gate at the bottom of the slope with a path beyond, leading down the side of the river.

CHAPTER 25

Nell reaches the gate well ahead of us, then stops and looks back, with obvious impatience. Bulleteyes and Greasy reach her and wait too, then Forkman and Meggie get there, and finally the three of us, Smarmy and Lippygirl still either side of me. They're watching me closely, though they must know I won't try anything while they've got Meggie too. Through the gate, and down the path by the river, away from the docks and the rest of the city, a horrible yawning space opening to my left where the water stretches away. I push the fear of it back and try to focus on what's happening. I've got to stay alert, just in case there's some way out of this.

Trouble is, I don't know what's down here, apart from a long walk to the sea. No people, certainly. Bulleteyes was right about that. It's like only ghosts live here, and they're going to have two more soon to add to their number. I plod on, staring about me, the path stretching ahead, the black river widening as we go, and dark, deserted timber yards to our right, separated from us by high metal fences. We're keeping together now as a group, apart from Nell, who's gone striding ahead again.

I stare at her as she pushes angrily forward, and then think back to the cul-de-sac, and my first glimpse of her there, and the realization of who she was, and what she was doing; and something sparks in my head, an image of her, in that scene; and I go on watching her, and thinking. But I don't get to think for long. Smarmy prods me suddenly.

'So what's with this wardrobe, Mikey?' he sniggers.

I don't answer.

'Couldn't help hearing Mumsy on the phone,' he goes on. He mimics Mum's voice. 'Mikey, please come out of the wardrobe, baby.'

I glance at him.

'She didn't say that.'

'Think she did, man. Word for word.'

'She didn't say baby.'

'But she meant baby, didn't she, Mikey?' he says. 'Yeah, she did, 'cos you's her little baby, ain't you? Like you're Meggie's little baby, too, right? Oh, yeah, we noticed. You're everybody's baby, ain't you, Mikey?'

I turn my eyes from his as they search my face for a reaction. Again, I see Nell pushing on ahead, the only person here who won't have heard this exchange; and there's that image again, of the cul-de-sac, and Nell in it. But Smarmy isn't finished.

'Come on, Mikey,' he says, 'you ain't told me. What's with the wardrobe?'

Again I don't answer. Smarmy leans close.

'Maybe you're just afraid of the big bad world.' He chuckles. 'But don't worry, Mikey, 'cos it's soon gonna be over. For both of you.'

I see Meggie look round at me, and there's that inward gaze again. I think of the courage she's always had but all I feel now is her despair. I don't know all the things they've done to her, and I don't think I can bear to know, but right now she looks broken, and if that's true, then maybe it's just as well they're going to kill us, because nothing's worth living for now, if Meggie's not right. I try to smile at her, but I can't, and she can't either. Smarmy gives another laugh.

'Ah, it's so cute watching you two,' he says, 'staring at each other, all gooey-eyed.'

I keep my voice low.

'How did you get her?'

'Oh, we're having a conversation now, are we?' says Smarmy.

'How did you get Meggie?'

I keep my eyes on her, but she's staring ahead. Don't know if she heard me just now. I hope not. To my relief, Smarmy plays along and leans close.

'Easy peasy, Mikey,' he says in a mock-confidential whisper. 'She just walked into our hands. Came out of school early all by herself. Too good a chance to miss. We just drove our car ahead of her, jumped out, and popped her in it. Just shows you shouldn't bunk off school, eh, Mikey? But maybe she wasn't doing that. Maybe she was heading home early to look after baby brother. What do you think?'

I go on staring at Meggie, guilt piling up again. The worst of it is this bastard's probably right. I know Meggie was worried about me. She'd texted Mum about it, and she probably got permission to go home early so she

146

could be there for me. She still doesn't look round, but Forkman does, and his face is all the warning I need to keep my distance from her. Smarmy chuckles again

'Say one thing for your sister, Mikey, she's a sparky little kid. Fought her corner good when we caught her. Till we trimmed her up a bit. Know what I mean?'

I round on him, lashing out, but he's ready, more than ready, because he's been goading me for this moment, longing for it, and now he's going to enjoy himself. He blocks my punches easily, trips me up with a hoot of laughter, then grins down at me on the ground.

'Yeah, Mikey,' he says, 'she fought her corner good. Much better than you, shithead.'

And he slams his boot into my ribs.

I roll over on the path, moaning. In the blackness I hear Meggie scream my name, but I'm already being hauled back to my feet by Smarmy and Lippygirl, and when I look round again, I see Bulleteyes and Greasy have walked on, with Forkman bundling Meggie after them, and Nell lost from view somewhere ahead. Smarmy and Lippygirl push themselves close again, each holding one of my arms.

'Let's go,' says Lippygirl.

She glances at Smarmy.

'And lay off him for a bit, or we'll never get it done.'

They push me down the path, and we walk on in silence, well behind the others now. I'm stepping faster, desperate to catch Meggie up, but Smarmy and Lippygirl sense that, and pull me back to the speed they want me to go. I don't suppose they really care what that is, as long as it's the opposite of what I want. I slow down.

There's no point resisting. I'll only end up on the ground again, and this time Smarmy will let rip, and Lippygirl won't stop him.

We walk on, the river still widening. It's a big black snake now, and it's twisting round to the right. The opposite shore is a mirror of this one: timber yards interspersed with patches of scrawny ground. More pillboxes here and there, and little broken-down huts, and even some rusty landing stages down on the river, with old lighters and barges moored, but nobody in them. Distant sound of traffic, and sometimes nothing at all, like the city has ceased to exist.

We're catching the others up, or maybe they're just slowing down. I can see Forkman with Meggie, and Bulleteyes and Greasy standing by them, Meggie a little apart, and all three checking her over. But they're not worried. Where's she going to run? And even if she could escape somewhere, they must know she wouldn't, with me in tow. I stare up at the sky, try to find something else to see. All dark up there, a huge blank vault. I gaze about me and wonder why I ever feared the open space. It seems nothing now compared with the fear of Meggie dying.

I fix my eyes on her again. She's turned in my direction and she's watching me approach with Smarmy and Lippygirl. I want to run ahead and throw my arms round her, and beg her to forgive me again, but I know they'll stop me, and make her suffer even more. I've got to keep calm somehow, in case there's some small chance to help Meggie. It doesn't matter about me. I'm nothing, but I've got to do everything I can for Meggie. She's all that matters now. She's all that has ever mattered. I walk on with Smarmy and Lippygirl, still a hundred yards or so from the others, and something tells me that this is where it's all going to end.

And it seems I'm right. The moment we join the others, everything changes. Smarmy and Lippygirl step apart from me, Forkman steps away from Meggie, the gang move round us on the path. I reach out and take Meggie's hand and squeeze it. I wait for hers to squeeze mine back, but it doesn't. It's limp. I peer into her face, and see to my horror that even the inward gaze has gone, and her eyes are closed. I look back at the gang, wondering how they're going to do this, then realize with a start that I've forgotten Nell. A moment later I hear her voice below us.

'Get 'em down here,' she yells, 'and hurry up!'

Still holding Meggie's hand, I turn to face the river and there, down some steps at the base of the wall, with the water lapping at her feet, is Nell. Moored beside her are two rowing boats.

CHAPTER 26

They push us towards the steps and follow, crowding round to block any escape. I make my way down, still holding Meggie's hand and watching her as she climbs passively down after me. Her eyes are open now, but they're without expression, even for me, and there's still no pressure in her hand. The gang are coming down after us, one by one. I glance back at the steps. The ones near the bottom are slippery and wet. Close by me, Nell's still fuming with impatience.

'Get a move on!' she shouts.

I catch her eye and see it harden, and even now the other image struggles to break through into my mind, the thing I saw in the cul-de-sac that night. As I grapple with the thought of it, her hand flicks out and cuffs me in the face.

'Get in the boat!' she says.

I stare down. Both the rowing boats are long and narrow and battered, but I can see which one's intended for us: it's the boat with the heavy chain coiled in the bottom. Nell's hand cuffs me again.

'I said, get in the boat!' She nods to the one with the chain. 'That one!'

I turn round to look at Meggie, then at the rest of the gang on the steps above. Something tells me Bulleteyes is the only one with any authority to change things now.

'Let Meggie go,' I call to him. 'She's got nothing to do with this.'

'Get her in the boat,' he says.

'Please.'

'Get her in the boat and shut your mouth.'

I feel a hand grab my shoulder and I know it's Nell. I turn and look at her. All I see is unrelenting rage. I search for some resemblance to Nip, or some quality that the two of them might share, but her face only hardens, and now she's yanking me towards the boat. I let go of Meggie's hand in case I slip on the wet stone and pull her down with me, and somehow lurch over the bottom step and into the boat.

'Sit there!' says Nell, pointing to the stern.

I sit down, watching Meggie again. Nell's making hurried gestures but Meggie doesn't seem to notice them and simply climbs into the boat without fuss, sits next to me, and closes her eyes again. I take her hand and stroke it, but now Forkman's in the boat too, and Smarmy, and they've taken an oar each, and Nell's climbed into the stern with us.

'Sit in the bottom,' she snaps at us.

I ease Meggie down on to the bottom boards with me, our backs to Forkman and Smarmy at the oars. Nell takes her place on the stern seat and glares down at us.

'Hold out your hands,' she says.

Neither of us move. She flicks open her knife and brandishes it in Meggie's face.

'I said, hold out your hands! Both of you!'

We hold out our hands. Nell puts the knife away, ties our wrists together with rope, then glances up at Bulleteyes, Greasy and Lippygirl, still standing on the steps.

'We'll wrap the chain round 'em when we're out there,' she says.

Bulleteyes nods.

'We'll follow in the other boat.'

Nell doesn't answer. She just glances at Forkman and Smarmy, then jerks her head in the direction of downriver. They push off from the bank and start to row. I don't look round to see which way we're going. I've got to think and there isn't much time, and all I've got to go on is what I saw in the cul-de-sac. To my dismay, Smarmy pipes up behind me.

'Hey, Mikey, take a peek over your shoulder.'

I don't look round. I've got to focus on Nell while I've still got a chance. I go on staring up at her, and beyond her at the steps in the wall we've just left behind, slipping away into the darkness. She's not watching me or Meggie. She's peering over our heads at whatever we're rowing towards, the thing Smarmy wants me to look at. He prompts me again.

'Mikey, check over your shoulder.'

Again, I try to catch Nell's eye. It doesn't even flicker in my direction, but something tells me she knows I'm watching her, maybe even wanting her attention. Her face hardens still further. I feel the fury boiling under her eyes. Smarmy calls out again, still taunting but working up some anger of his own now.

'Turn round, Mikey, or Sis gets my oar in her back.'

I turn round and see him grinning at me, even as he goes on rowing. Next to him Forkman works his own oar and looks on in silence.

'Good boy, Mikey!' says Smarmy. 'See? That wasn't difficult, was it? Now look over the bow. That's the pointy bit at the front. What do you see?'

I hear the splash of other oars nearby where Bullet-eyes, Greasy, and Lippygirl are catching us up in the other boat. Forkman glances across at them but Smarmy keeps his eyes on my face.

'What do you see, Mikey?'

'An old barge moored in the middle of the river.'

'Well done, Mikey! Good lad!'

I turn quickly back to face the stern, but nothing's changed. Nell's still staring over the top of me in the direction of the barge. Meggie hasn't moved, except to dip her head over her bound wrists. I glance over the water to my left and see the other boat just a short distance away. I look up at Nell again and I know I've got to try this. It's our only hope and it's got to be now. To my annoyance, Smarmy's voice comes leering back.

'That's your new home, Mikey,' he says, 'you and Sis. Well, not the barge. You ain't going to be on that. You're going to be underneath it. Ain't that fun? The two of you wrapped up in pretty chains, lying together on the river-bed, underneath the boat. You can look right up its arse, if you want to, only maybe not. 'Cos it's a deep part of the river there, Mikey. Did you know that? Really, really deep. Ah, well, we're going to be sorry to lose you, but the thing is, Mikey, we got no choice 'cos you know too much. So we gotta put you somewhere no one can find you. No traces, yeah? But I'll tell you something. Gonna break my heart, man, when you and Sis go over the side. I might even have to look the other way. Know what I mean?'

He falls silent, at last, and I fix my eyes on Nell. She goes on gazing beyond me. I think of the moored barge, drawing closer with every stroke. A minute, two minutes, maybe that's all we've got now, Meggie and me; and all I've got to make something happen. Nell's still staring past me, as though she doesn't want to meet my eyes. I lean towards the stern, look up into her angry face, and lower my voice.

'Nell,' I murmur.

CHAPTER 27

She doesn't answer. But she heard me. Smarmy and Forkman didn't, but she did. I try again, more urgently.

'Nell.'

Her eyes dart down at me.

'Don't talk to me, shitboy.'

'You're not like them, Nell.'

'Shut your mouth.'

'You're trying to be but you're not.'

'You deaf?'

Her hand whips out and slaps me in the face. I hear Smarmy laugh behind me, and even Forkman, but the splash of the oars goes on. The sound of the other boat seems louder suddenly, but I don't dare look away from Nell to see where it is. I stare up at the face glowering down at me and force myself to speak again, in the same low voice.

'You stood back, Nell.'

'Shut it,' says Nell.

'In the cul-de-sac. I saw you. I remember it. You stood back. You didn't want to be there.'

'Shut it, I said!'

'The others killed the old man. You didn't.'

'Shut it!' she screams, and she lashes out again, this time with her fist. It thuds into the side of my face and for a moment I feel my vision go; then, to my relief, it flickers back. I see Meggie next to me push her wrists into her face, her body shuddering against mine. I hear shouts from the other boat.

'What's going on?' roars Bulleteyes.

Smarmy calls back to him.

'Nell's got the hump with the boy!'

'What about?'

'Don't know. Does it matter?'

'Nell!' calls Lippygirl. 'What's going on?'

I see Nell glance across the water, then back at me, her eyes crazed.

'You're not like them, Nell,' I say quickly. 'You're just trying to be.'

'Shut your mouth, shitboy!'

'You didn't want to kill the old man and you don't want to kill us.'

'Shut your mouth!'

'You hated what was happening in the cul-de-sac. I could see it. You hated every moment of it.'

I feel the words coming faster and faster.

'And you're hating this too, because you know it's wrong. You're acting hard because the others don't believe in you and you want to prove yourself, but for what? The old man who died had twenty quid in his wallet. That's all. His wife said he just went out for a walk. I heard it on the news. And your friends still kicked him to death. Is that what you wanted? And now me and

Meggie? Is that what Nip would want you to do? Nip's the only reason I didn't report you in the first place. I wanted to protect your little brother.'

'Stop!' she says.

'And now you want to kill me and my little sister.'

'Stop!'

'Nip wouldn't want this, Nell.'

'Shut it!'

'He wouldn't.'

'Shut your mouth!'

'But you don't care about Nip, do you?'

'Shut the—'

'Because if you really loved him, Nell, you'd help us.'

'Stop! Stop! Stop!'

Nell plunges a hand into her pocket, then strikes out again. I feel a hissing pain in my cheek, then blood oozing down my face. I stare down in horror and watch it run over my chest. When I look up again, I see the flick knife, red and moist, and Nell's eyes staring. Behind me I hear the oars fall silent, then Forkman's voice.

'What's going on, Nell?'

She's still staring, but the fire has gone from her eyes, and something else has taken its place. I don't know what. I try to think of something to say, but I can't find any words. Then, in a distant voice, Meggie speaks.

'Nell,' she says, 'please help us.'

Voices are now bawling across the water at us: Lippygirl, Greasy, and Bulleteyes all shouting to know what's going on, and someone behind me's stood up, maybe both the guys, because the boat's rocking from side to side. I keep my eyes on Nell, but she's not looking at me at all. She's watching Meggie with a strange, almost frightened expression; then suddenly she lunges again with her knife.

'No!' I yell.

But it's not to stab: it's to hack at the ropes round our wrists. I hear more shouts from the other boat, and from Smarmy and Forkman too.

'Nell!'

'Nell!'

'What's happened?'

'What you doing?'

But they've seen now.

'Stop her!' shouts Bulleteyes.

The ropes fall from our wrists and Nell stands up in the boat, her eyes wild.

'I can't do it,' she mutters, 'I can't do it.'

'Tie 'em up again,' yells Bulleteyes.

I turn to see Forkman stumbling towards us, the boat heaving as he shoulders Smarmy out of the way, and now he's reaching towards Meggie. Nell steps over me without a word and slashes at him with her knife. He gives a moan and falls back on to the coil of chain, blood spouting from his neck. I stand up, grab Meggie by the hand, and tug her to her feet. She stares at me for a moment, then seems to understand, and without resistance lets me pull her with me over the side. As we splash into the river, I hear the shot.

But there's no time to think of it. The coldness and blackness of the water force everything from me but the need to save Meggie, and already I've lost her. In spite of my efforts, her hand has slipped away. I flounder to the surface and look for her. There's no sign of her at all, just the two boats drifting a few yards away, all the gang members on their feet, apart from Forkman, who's hidden from view, and Nell, slumped over near the stern. Smarmy's staring at her, his gun drawn. Then Meggie breaks the surface close by.

'Meggie,' I gasp.

She sees me and draws breath. I struggle towards her, but my clothes are weighing me down and I can see hers are doing the same. I reach her somehow and take her hand again.

'Meggie,' I murmur, 'we've got to swim to the old barge. We won't make it to the shore. It's too far.'

She doesn't answer and I'm frightened she's giving up again.

'Can you do that, Meggie?' I say.

She lets go of my hand, and starts to swim towards the barge. I follow, still fighting the weight of my clothes and unsure whether to stop and pull them off in case the cold makes things worse. Behind us, the air is full of shouts. I glance over my shoulder. The two boats are together now and Bulleteyes and Greasy have climbed over into the one Meggie and I were in, and they're checking over Forkman, who's now half-upright. No one's bothering with Nell. She's hauled herself on to the stern seat again, but she's slumped over, her head down, the bleach-blonde hair bright against her chest.

Meggie's losing strength already and so am I. I check the old barge. We're nearly there and I think the tide's helping us, but we've got to be careful not to get washed past or we won't be able to swim back. More weary strokes, and now the pain from my knife wound is starting to tell. I don't know how much blood I've lost but if I don't reach the boat soon, I'll black out, and I must stay conscious for Meggie's sake. She's making a last effort, splashing doggedly on, and I see something of her old spirit in those frantic strokes. I drive myself after her, determined to stay close, and now we're almost there. I can see the ugly mooring buoy, the hawser stretching upwards, the black hull tugging against it. I call out to Meggie.

'Swim for the buoy first.'

But she's already doing so. A moment later she's there.

'Grab anything you can,' I call, 'and don't let go.'

I see her hand clutch a section of the hawser.

'Hold it tight, Meggie.'

Already the tide is trying to sweep her past the buoy, but she clings on, and a moment later I'm there too. I reach out and grab the hawser, and we hang there, our bodies pushed together by the tide, both of us shivering and in as much danger from the cold now as we were from the gang. But the gang haven't gone—and they've got unfinished business. The boats have separated again, and one is now heading this way. I reach out with my free hand and slip my arm round Meggie's shoulder. Maybe it's because I always knew deep down that this was just a stay of execution; and I may not get a chance to touch Meggie again. I pull her close, kiss the top of her head. She's shivering worse than ever now, and so am I, and the pain from my wound is growing worse, but I don't care about that. I kiss Meggie again.

'I'm sorry, Meggie,' I say, and I turn back to watch the boat.

It's the one we were in, only now it's got the whole gang, apart from Nell. I don't know where she is. I can see the other boat further off, drifting by itself, but there's no sign of Nell in it, so they've either dumped her in the bottom or rolled her into the river. I look back at the approaching boat. Forkman's sitting in the stern, Lippygirl bent over him, something pressed to his wound. Smarmy and Greasy are at the oars. Bulleteyes is up in the bow, glowering ahead at us.

I feel something cold touch my hip. It startles me for a moment, then I realize what it is. I look round and into Meggie's face. She's put her arm round my waist. Her face is as blank as it was before, but I can feel what she's trying to say. I kiss her again, and turn back to Bulleteyes. He's just a short distance away now and the oars have stopped pulling. He stares down at me, and even in his anger, manages a sneer.

'Well, posh boy,' he says, 'you've been a real pain in the arse, haven't you? But at least you done us a favour. You've saved us the trouble of rowing you over here. Just as well we didn't lose the chain in all that fuss, eh? And you done us another favour too. Shown us we needed to get rid of Nell. Like we suspected. So thanks, mate. Nice work.'

The others are crowding forward now, Greasy and Smarmy and Lippygirl and even Forkman, with a bloody shirt clapped to his wound. It's as though they all want a last gloat. I feel Meggie's hand again, pressing me gently. With my own I pull her closer still. Bulleteyes snaps his fingers and the others start to move. Forkman returns to the stern. Smarmy sits back at the oars and starts to ease the boat towards the buoy. Greasy and Lippygirl bend down and a moment later straighten up, holding the heavy chain. Bulleteyes stays in the bow, grinning down at us.

And that's when I hear the sound of the police launch.

CHAPTER 28

Things happen fast after that, but I only remember flashes because I keep blacking out. I remember the beam from the launch drowning us in light, the voice in the loudhailer, the shouts from the gang, the sight of them rowing frantically down the river. I remember the other boat drifting as before, and wondering about Nell, worrying about Nell, and about Meggie, because she's slipping down in the water, and I want to hold her up. Only I'm slipping too. I remember the feeling of cold and numbness in my body, and the rain starting, and lights moving on both banks of the river, and then figures reaching down to us. I can't remember if they lowered a boat and rowed across or just hauled us up into the launch. I just remember being in a cabin with Meggie, and more figures around us, and then Meggie being taken somewhere else, and I'm being helped out of my wet clothes, and I can hear the roar of an engine, and I think it's the launch revving up, and then it's black again.

And the next time I look up, it's into Mum's face, and Dad's face, and I'm dry and in a bed somewhere, and they're telling me it's the hospital; but I'm still worrying about Meggie, and about Nell, and a man I don't know appears and says it's OK, but I don't know what he means, and then it's black again. Next time I wake up, I see Mum and Dad still watching me, and the man who spoke to me before, and they're telling me he's Doctor Somebody, and he says I'm going to be all right because they've checked over my injuries and dressed the wound in my face and sorted the stitches and everything, and although I'm going to be hurting for a while and I'll need follow-up checks, I can go home when I've had another good rest. But then I fall asleep again and the next time I wake, it's just Dad with me in the ward.

'What time is it?' I say.

'Eleven in the morning,' he says. 'You've been in the hospital overnight, but you've slept most of the time, which is good.'

'How's Meggie?'

'She's at home with your mum. They went back an hour ago. The doctors have checked her injuries and given her medication, but they think she'll be much better off with her family and her own things around her. And they said the same applies to you, Mikey, so the sooner you're back home too, the happier your mum and I will be.'

'But how is Meggie?' I say. 'You haven't told me.'

'She was badly beaten up, Mikey,' says Dad, 'but Doctor Williams has told us she'll come through the physical injuries in a few weeks. The psychological injuries are harder to predict, so if you ask me how she's feeling inside, Mikey, I have to say I don't know right now. What I do know, what we both know, is that Meggie's a strong character, and we have to just hope that's what pulls her through.'

Dad leans close suddenly and puts his hand on my cheek, the side that wasn't slashed by the knife.

'And you'll pull through too, Mikey,' he says. 'I can't tell you how proud of you I am, and how proud of you your mum is.'

'I don't know why,' I say. 'I've messed up so badly. I've caused all this trouble, including what's happened to Meggie.'

Dad shakes his head.

'Let's not think about blame,' he says. 'Let's think about getting you and Meggie well again, and our family back together.'

'OK.'

'Good lad.'

He gives my shoulder a squeeze.

'Dad?'

'Yes, Mikey?'

'Does my face look terrible?'

'Well, it never was that good.'

'Don't make jokes, Dad.'

'You look fine, Mikey.'

'What about the knife wound?'

Dad frowns.

'So it was a knife,' he says. 'DI Paget said she thought it must have been done by a blade.' He shakes his head. 'Oh, Mikey, you've really been through it, haven't you? You must tell us all what happened as soon as you feel strong enough. I know DI Paget's keen to speak to you.'

'I'm ready to speak now.'

'Are you sure?'

'Yes,' I say, 'but you still haven't told me what the wound looks like.'

'I can't see it,' he says. 'It's covered by the dressing.'

'But you saw it before, didn't you?'

'No,' says Dad, 'the medics had you patched up before they let us see you. But I've been told . . . ' He hesitates. 'I've been told it's a deep cut.'

'Will it go when it's healed up?'

'I don't know,' he says. 'We'll have to ask Doctor Williams.'

Dad looks at me for a moment, then gives my shoulder another squeeze.

'I'm so sorry, Mikey,' he says. 'A knife scar on top of everything else.'

'I suppose it might give me some respect at school.'

'True.'

'And I could do with a bit of that there. I don't normally get much.'

Dad laughs.

'I'll certainly be surprised if anyone calls you Mole again,' he says, 'but actually I think you're wrong about the respect thing. You may find you're more popular than you realize at school. If it hadn't been for some of the staff and pupils, the police might never have been able to trace you.'

'What do you mean?'

'Apparently,' says Dad, 'some of your fellow students spotted two figures on a motorbike hovering by the school gate watching you while you got into the car that time to go home with your mum, and then following when you set off. They thought the two figures were act-ing suspiciously and reported it to Mrs Warby. And the caretaker . . . what's his name?'

'Mr Fenby.'

'Mr Fenby reported that he'd seen a dodgy-looking boy and girl peering over the top of the playground wall and staring across at Room Eighteen—'

'Which I was in,' I say. 'I saw them watching me.'

'I don't think anyone thought much of it at the time,' says Dad. 'There was no obvious connection with you. But clearly, some people must have carried on talking about it, because later, after you went off on your own, we got a call from Mr Cable.'

'Mr Cable?'

'Yes,' says Dad. 'He rang us to ask if you were all right. Said he and Mrs Reed had both been worrying about you because you'd seemed frightened at school, and then he mentioned the girl and the boy Mr Fenby had seen. That meant nothing to us, of course, but the moment he told us about the guys on the motorbike following the car, your mum remembered the two who had hovered close by you on your way back from school, and your V-sign to them, and we rang the police.'

As if on cue, two policewomen appear by the bedside.

'Is this a bad time?' says one.

'Not at all,' says Dad. 'Mikey, this is DI Paget and this is . . .'

He looks blankly at the other officer.

'DC Bellingham,' she says.

'Michael,' says DI Paget, 'how are you feeling?'

'OK,' I murmur.

She draws up a chair and her colleague does the same. 'Are you well enough to talk to us, Michael?'

'Yes,' I say, 'I really want to. And I want to know about Nell.'

CHAPTER 29

DI Paget glances at her colleague, then back at me.

'We'll answer your questions in due course, Michael,' she says, 'but let's hear your bit first.'

I start with what I saw in the cul-de-sac, and who, and how I had a chance to run away and didn't, and how the gang saw me, and the messages started, and the threats. How the game changed when I put my face to that gap in the fence.

'You should have told us all this, Mikey,' says Dad, 'and the police.'

'I was frightened of what the gang would do,' I say. 'I know it was wrong, but I was scared, and I was worried for Nip too, because of Nell being involved in a murder. I know she didn't do the murder herself—she just kind of stood there and let the others do it—but I got confused about what to do, and then they came looking for me, and now Meggie's been hurt and—'

'Let's hear the rest, Michael,' says DI Paget. 'But take your time.'

I tell her everything I can remember up to the moment the police launch arrived.

'You were very brave, Michael,' she says, 'and so was your sister.'

'But how did you know where we were?' I say.

'It was easier than you think,' says the officer. 'We had good enough descriptions of the two gang members Mr Fenby saw to identify the individuals concerned. The motorbike riders completed the picture. This gang have been well known to us for some time, including Nell. We didn't know what they were up to this time but we knew they often hang out by the docks and use the old pillboxes to meet up in, and sometimes go on the river in rowing boats, so when we received a separate report from a bus driver telling us he'd dropped off an anxious-looking boy who matched your description by the lane that leads down to the docks, we got moving. We knew the gang were very dangerous.'

DI Paget pauses for a moment, then goes on.

'And what you've now told us about the incident in the cul-de-sac, Michael, is a critical piece of information in this murder inquiry, so we're very grateful for that. We'll need to take a full statement from you as soon as you're able to provide it.'

'How did the gang get Mikey's email and mobile details?' says Dad.

'Nell will have got all that for them,' says the officer. 'She'll have taken it from her brother's computer or mobile phone and passed it on. The home address too. I don't imagine Nip knew anything about it.'

'So what's happened to the gang?' I say.

'They rowed off down the river,' she says, 'but we were accompanied by a second police launch, which you

170

probably didn't see, and we also had backup from operatives onshore, so we had no problem rounding everyone up. The gang members are now in custody.'

'And Nell?'

The policewoman frowns.

'Nell was touch and go for a while, Michael,' she says quietly. 'She was shot, as you've described, and we found her lying in the bottom of the second rowing boat. She very nearly died on her way to the hospital, but she made it somehow; they've now operated on her, and we think she's going to pull through. Her family are with her right now.'

I feel a sudden, desperate pain.

'If it hadn't been for her,' I say, 'if it hadn't . . . '

I look away, picturing Nell's harsh, aggressive face as the anger turned into something else, and the game changed for her too. Then I think of someone I'm more desperate to see than anybody in the world.

'I want to see Meggie,' I murmur.

'I know, Mikey,' says Dad, 'and you soon will.'

But it's not soon enough for me. There's more talking with DI Paget, and then Doctor Williams, and last medical checks before they can discharge me, and while all that's going on, Dad disappears to ring Mum; somehow, eventually, I'm dressed and it's just me and Dad walking together to the door of the hospital. I glance at him.

'Did you speak to Meggie on the phone just now?'

'No, only your mum.'

'Is Meggie all right?'

'She's back where she belongs,' says Dad, 'and that's the main thing.'

171

I give him a quizzical look but he ignores it and goes on.

'Mikey, I've told your mum everything you said to me and DI Paget, so she's got the full story of what happened, OK? You don't need to repeat the whole thing when you get home.'

Dad stops suddenly.

'I'm not parked very near the entrance, Mikey. Do you want to wait here while I go and bring the car closer?'

I check out the sunlight.

'It's a bit bright,' says Dad. 'Let me go and get the car.'

'No,' I say, 'we can walk.'

'Are you sure?'

I set off without a word, and we're soon outside, but my good intentions crumble as the light cuts into me and the space yawns all around.

'Where are you parked?' I mutter.

'Over there.'

I peer through the blinding cloud and see the car in the far corner.

'OK, Dad.'

I lurch towards it, fighting the urge to run, but at last I'm there.

'Do you want to get in the back?' says Dad.

'No, the front.'

'Are you sure?'

'Yes, for God's sake.'

He unlocks the doors and I dive in. The light's growing sharper, more painful, and for some reason the knife wound feels worse too. I click on the safety belt, close my eyes, force them open again, and stare out through the windscreen.

'Is it still terrible?' says Dad, next to me.

'I didn't feel it so bad yesterday,' I say, 'when I was out looking for Meggie. It wasn't just because it was dark and I'm better when there's no sunlight. I still get panicky in the dark when it's somewhere I don't know, and if there's a lot of space, but the whole feeling I usually get of being . . . eaten . . . swallowed . . . I don't know . . . it just wasn't as bad yesterday. But it's come flooding back again now.'

Dad starts the engine.

'The sooner we get you home the better,' he says.

We drive back in silence, and somehow, the sharpness of the light starts to ease. Maybe it's because my mind's fixed on Meggie again. I'm yearning to see her now, not just because I want to say sorry again, but because I can tell something else has happened, something unexpected, something Dad doesn't want to talk about. We reach Denbury Close and pull over in front of the house. I unclick the safety belt and lean back in the seat, trying to calm my thoughts. Dad switches off the engine and leans back too.

'Mikey,' he says, 'you know why you didn't feel the old fears so much when you were looking for Meggie yesterday? Because greater fears overwhelmed them. It's how nature helps us survive.'

'What do you mean?'

'It often happens in an emergency. We're forced to confront the greatest danger, and we push aside our smaller fears in order to do so. But once the big danger is past, the smaller fears come back again.'

'So I'm always going to be weak.'

'You're not weak, Mikey,' says Dad, 'you're strong, you're very strong, and you may find, you know, that these smaller fears are losing their grip on you even now. I'm convinced that the more you look them in the face and stand up to them, the way you stood up so bravely to those gang members, the more you'll find they'll gradually lose their power to hurt you.'

I look at him, then shake my head.

'Why can't Mr Braine ever say things that way?'

'Because the man's a dickhead,' says Dad, 'and we're not going to use him any more.' He smiles, but is quickly serious again. 'Mikey, listen,' he goes on, 'you asked me earlier if Meggie's all right and I didn't really answer you.'

'I know.'

But I've worked out the reason. Dad doesn't need to say any more. I glance round at the house and see Mum watching us from the front room window. There's no sign of Meggie, and I understand why. I look back at Dad.

'I know what's happened, Dad.'

'I don't think you do, Mikey.'

'I know what's happened,' I say. 'I've guessed.'

I've got to go in now. I don't need Dad's explanation. I can't wait any longer. I must see Meggie. I jump out of the car and run to the house. Mum already has the front door open, and she hurries out and throws her arms round me.

'Mikey,' she says, 'I'm so glad you're back.'

'I love you, Mum.'

'I love you too.'

'And him,' I say, nodding at Dad as he walks up after me. 'I love him too.'

Dad puts his arms round both of us, and we stand there in a huddle for a few moments, then I ease myself free.

'I've got to see Meggie.'

'Mikey, listen,' says Mum.

'I know what's happened, Mum, OK?'

'Dad's told you?'

'No, I've worked it out. Can I go up?'

Mum and Dad look at each other, then back at me.

'Go ahead, Mikey,' says Dad.

I step into the house and walk up the stairs, and straight away feel that quietness again, the quietness of Denbury Close, as though nothing has ever changed here, and the silent lives in these silent houses are carrying on as they've always done, and probably always will. The stairs are silent, the landing's silent. I don't go into Meggie's room. I turn straight into my own, and here's the familiar space, the familiar bed, the familiar bookshelves, only some of my favourite titles are missing. I wasn't expecting that. But I know where they are. I turn to the wardrobe and open the door. Meggie stares out at me from the darkness within. She's curled up in the left-hand corner, books sprawled around her, unopened, one large volume in her hand, also unopened. I kneel down and look in at her, then at the book in her hand.

'*Moby Dick*,' I say. 'Good choice, Meggie.'

She says nothing. I reach in, push the other books out of the way to make space for myself, then crawl inside and squeeze next to her. There's only just room for the two of us, but it's not uncomfortable. I pull the door slowly to and darkness closes around us. Meggie turns her head towards me. Her face looks ghost-like, but the bruises are still visible, and the pain inside her—that's visible too.

'I'm sorry, Meggie,' I whisper.

She doesn't answer.

'Meggie, please tell me there's a chance you'll forgive me one day.'

She puts down the book and takes my hand.

'It's all right, Mikey,' she says.

'It's not all right,' I say, 'but I want to make it all right if I can.'

She strokes my hand, just once.

'How did they catch you?' I say.

'I got permission to leave school early.'

'To come home and look after me?'

'Yes.'

'And they pushed you into a car?'

'Yes.'

Just as Smarmy said, the bastard. I squeeze Meggie's hand gently.

'I got a text with the words: I love you, big guy. Only it wasn't spelt the way you'd write it. Was it from you?'

'The girl with the piercings wrote it,' she says. 'They wanted me to send you a text but they didn't want me to write it in case I sent another message. So I had to dictate it and the girl wrote it and sent it.' Meggie looks down. 'But it was from me, Mikey. And I meant what I said.'

'I love you too, Meggie. I love you so much.'

'I know that, Mikey. It's all right.' She looks down. 'Is Nell dead?'

'She's going to pull through. She was touch and go but she's going to be OK.'

Meggie starts to cry. I go on squeezing her hand.

'Meggie, I feel so terrible,' I say, 'because I've caused all this. You haven't heard the whole story yet and I'll tell you another time, but it's all been my fault. I don't know how I can ever put things right, but I want to so much. You've got to believe me.'

She lets go of my hand, slips an arm round me, and we hold each other in the darkness, and after a while she stops crying. The silence goes on around us, and deepens, but we stay where we are, holding on to each other; then, some minutes later, I hear Mum and Dad on the stairs, then on the landing, then outside my room. But they don't come in. Meggie and I pull apart and look at each other. I reach up and stroke her face.

'Are you ready, Meggie?' I say.

She takes a long, heavy breath, then nods.

'Let's go, then,' I say.

And I open the door of the wardrobe, take Meggie by the hand again, and help her out.

Tim Bowler is one of the UK's most compelling and original writers for teenagers. He was born in Leigh-on-Sea and after studying Swedish at university, he worked in forestry, the timber trade, teaching, and translating before becoming a full-time writer. He lives with his wife in a quiet Devon village and his workroom is a small wooden outhouse known to friends as 'Tim's Bolthole'.

Tim has written twenty books and won fifteen awards, including the prestigious Carnegie Medal for *River Boy*, and his provocative *BLADE* series is being hailed as a groundbreaking work of fiction. He has been described by the *Sunday Telegraph* as 'the master of the psychological thriller' and by the *Independent* as 'one of the truly individual voices in British teenage fiction'. His books have sold over a million copies worldwide.

www.timbowler.co.uk

Also by TiM BOWLER,
the breathtaking . . .

Turn the page
for a piece of the action . . .

I step out of the phone box, aware of the guy's hand on m shoulder. It's not gripping me, but I can feel the pressu guiding me towards the car. I walk towards it and feel t hand leave. I stop and it comes back, light but firm. I walk and the hand leaves again. Closer now, to the open door.

The guys in the front aren't watching me. They're ju staring ahead, like they're not interested, like this is no k deal. Maybe it isn't, to them. I stop again, feel the ha return. I look round into Flash Coat's face. The mouth smiling again, but the eyes are colder than ever. The ha stays on my shoulder, and now it squeezes.

'Get in, boy,' he says.

I hear a car horn close by. The hand lets go but stays clo: I look round at the street. There's a taxi trying to pull out little way down, but another car's cut across him and he stuck. Another blast from the taxi. The other guy gives hi the finger. I look up at Flash Coat. He's checking them, n me.

I duck under his arm and tear off down the street. I don look round, just keep running. No idea what's going on behin me, then I hear the engine. A soft purr, just to my right, and moment later I see the bonnet of the car edge alongside m keeping pace. Same as before: neither of the men looking me. I check the back of the car.

Flash Coat's not there.

I cut left, into the garage forecourt, run across to the fa thest pump, stop, look round. The car's pulled to the side the street, ticking over quietly as the traffic roars past it. I se the taxi overtake and disappear in the throng. The guys i the front are staring ahead, but here's Flash Coat walking u behind them.

Sauntering even, like there's no rush, like he doesn't war to crinkle his coat. No question he's the guy in control. H stops by the car, leans down. Nearside window opens, guy i the passenger seat says something, Flash Coat straightens up, looks over at me, and now he's sauntering again, this way.

I run round the back of the garage, past the car wash, past the pressure gauge, down to the end of the fence, stop by the gap. It's only small and it'll mess up my school uniform, but I don't care about that. What matters is that bastard's coat. He won't want to squeeze through with that thing on.

He might not even see where I've gone, if I'm quick. He hasn't appeared yet. I push through the gap, and now I'm on the other side of the fence and belting into Ashgrove Park. Only now I can see the car again. It's over to the right, tracking round the street. No sign of Flash Coat but the guy in the passenger seat's watching me through the park railings and talking on his phone.

This isn't going to work. Park's too small and there's only a scrawny little patch of grass and the children's playground and then I'm out in the street again. I stop by the water fountain where the path forks. The car pulls over to the side of the road, the guy still peering at me and talking on his phone.

I'm thinking of Flash Coat again. He's not behind me or following the car. I check the paths in front of the fountain. Seems pretty obvious suddenly. Right fork takes me back to the main road and the guys in the car will cover that. Left fork takes me to the Barrow Street exit, and that's where Flash Coat'll be waiting. Nothing else for it.

I turn and run back towards the broken fence. The guys in the car'll see what I'm doing but I've got to chance it. I might just get through the gap and away before Flash Coat changes direction and comes back. And the guys in the car won't get there for a good few minutes. They can't turn in the road where they are. They'll have to head down to the roundabout before they can cut back.

But even as I race towards the fence, I hear a blare of car horns and—shit! The guys in the car aren't bothering with the

roundabout. They've seen what I'm doing and they've ju
pulled straight out into the road, blocking cars, taxis, buse
everybody. More horns, a great shriek of noise from both sid
of the carriageway, but the car's still pulling across, and turn
ing, turning, and now they're round and tearing back towar
the garage.

I run on towards the fence, feeling the car in the corn
of my eye. They've slowed down again so they can keep n
in view, but they'll lose sight of me for about a minute on
I'm through the gap, and that's when I've got to decide—o
through the garage or back into the park.

I dive through the gap, stop, take a breath, dive back, ar
now I'm racing into the park again. No idea if this is the rig
thing to do. Glance to the right: no sign of the car. If they'v
guessed I've doubled back, it'll still take them a few momen
to turn again and come after me. What's bothering me no
is Flash Coat. He could be anywhere. I push him out of m
head and run on.

Water fountain.

Right fork. Obvious choice. Quickest way out of the par
and if I can just get to the main road before anyone stops m
I should be able to run over to the other side and lose ther
down one of the side streets. Past the children's playground
couple of mothers in there with toddlers in the sandpit, an
on towards the gate at the end.

The traffic goes on roaring past to my right, and I'm watch
ing it as I run, checking for the shiny car. No sign of it yet, bu
they'll have worked out by now that I'm not by the garag
and if they got there quick enough to be sure I didn't escap
that way, they'll be haring back here again. I glance over m
shoulder: still no car.

But now I've seen Flash Coat.

Standing in the gate ahead.

I stop, panting for breath. He's just watching, with tha

same expression of cool amusement he had back at the phone box. Doesn't bother walking into the park, just pulls out his mobile, taps a number, says a few words, puts his phone away—and there's that smile again. The one that comes from his mouth. I don't look at his eyes. I've already turned and I'm running again, back towards the fountain.

I don't bother checking the main road or back at him. Makes no difference now. They've got me covered whichever way I go. I take the other fork at the water fountain and tear off towards the Barrow Street exit. I won't get out that way. I already know it. Some part of me has given up. The part that's still thinking knows Flash Coat will stay where he is, one of the guys from the car will watch the gap in the fence, and the other one'll be waiting for me at Barrow Street. So there's no point in running.